only to discover . . .
Yay, ping-pong and good times!
and now . . .
I must bring balance back to The Force.
but not really.

THE LAST KIDS ON EARTH

AND THE ZOMBIE PARADE

MAX BRALLIER

ILLUSTRATED by DOUGLAS HOLGATE

EGMONT

We bring stories to life

First published in the United States of America by Viking,
an imprint of Penguin Random House LLC, 2016

This edition published in 2016
By Egmont UK Limited
The Yellow Building, 1 Nicholas Road, London W11 4AN

Text copyright © 2016 Max Brallier
Illustrations copyright © 2016 Douglas Holgate

The moral rights of the author and illustrator have been asserted.

ISBN 978 1 4052 8164 5

www.egmont.co.uk

63746/1

A CIP catalogue record for this title is available from the British Library

Printed and bound in Great Britain by CPI Group

Stay safe online. Any website addresses listed in this book are correct
at the time of going to print. However, Egmont is not responsible
for content hosted by third parties. Please be aware that online content
can be subject to change and websites can contain content
that is unsuitable for children. We advise that all children are
supervised when using the internet.

MIX
Paper
FSC FSC® C018306

To Ruby. If the world crumbled and the monsters were a-comin', you would make for a fantastic partner in adventure.

— M. B.

For my parents: For not only supporting, loving, and encouraging me at every turn, but also dropping me off regularly at the next-door neighbours who unbeknownst to you put me in front of pretty much every horror movie available at the video store when I was eight.

— D. H.

chapter one

OK, so . . . we are going to be eaten. Devoured.
Swallowed whole. Or maybe swallowed in bits.
Really, whole or bits? Does it matter? Bottom
line: EATEN.

'Cause see that train-sized beast behind us?

It's *not* a train. It's a humongo worm monster. The Wormungulous.

Now, *why* are we running from a humongo worm monster?

A very good question.

With a very silly answer. We are . . .

See, about a month ago, I defeated this big evil beast named Blarg. So I was like, 'We're heroes! Post-Apocalyptic Action Heroes. And Post-Apocalyptic Action Heroes *need* quests!'

We're basically the modern version of old-timey King Arthur-y knights. And old-timey King Arthur-y knights were always questing all over the place. That was when my best friend, Quint Baker, declared, 'We should build a bestiary, friend!'

What's a bestiary, you ask?

Also a good question! I asked Quint the same thing. Quint looked at me like I was completely brain-dead, grabbed the dictionary, and read, *'An illustrative, encyclopedic compendium detailing a myriad of mythical creatures.'*

'That just sounds like a fancy way of saying "monster notebook",' I said.

'But better!' Quint said. '"Notebook" implies school and study. "Bestiary" implies BEASTS. A book filled with crinkly yellow pages that smell of ancient history.'

I was def digging that, so I said . . .

And now we're building a *complete* bestiary of *every single strange creature* that has arrived in the town of Wakefield after the Monster Apocalypse began this past summer. You need two things for a bestiary entry:

One: a picture. That's my job. You *know* that's my job 'cause I'm Jack Sullivan, monster photographer *extraordinaire*.

Two: you need INFO. Like stuff about the monster – strengths, weaknesses, where does it hang, what does it eat, what are its hobbies, does it stink like evil, yadda, yadda, yadda.

Now, I realize in terms of, like, all-time ultimate heroic quests, 'writing a book' doesn't exactly rank up there with Frodo carrying the ring to Mount Doom, but whatever. I learned that just by calling *any* random old chore a quest, you can make life a LOT more fun.

For example . . .

I'm not picking my nose –

I'm on a quest to retrieve a long-dormant hunk of snot!

Heroically!

Separately, our friend Dirk's quest is to build a vegetable garden. That's not a joke. Dirk apparently loves fresh tomatoes. He says he can't maintain his hulking mass by surviving on Wotsits and Snickers alone. Which is BONKERS, since I'm pretty sure those are major food groups.

Dirk's part of my monster-fighting crew. He was a terrifying bully back before the end of the world, but now he's a terrifying monster-crushing man . . . with a soft side, as you can tell from his vegetable garden quest.

Dirk told us that if he had some tomatoes, he could probably make some bootleg pizzas over a fire. And I haven't had pizza – legit *or* bootleg – in months.

June Del Toro (who is kind of my favourite girl in the world) was in agreement with Dirk on this – she was dying for some non-junk food. Buncha crazies, if you ask me.

Anyway, these two very epic quests are the reason Quint, June, Dirk, and I are at the Circle One Mall right now. It's the reason we're racing down the mall's main corridor. It's the reason we're being chased by the Wormungulous. It's the reason –

KA-KA-KRASSSSH!!!

I crane my neck as my feet pound the floor.
Ah, fisticuffs – it's catching up!

My heart is slamming against my rib cage as
I race around the corner, past the fancy-pants
Belgian Godiva Chocolatier store, past the

Build-A-Bear Workshop, and past the always-tasty Millie's Cookies stall.

Suddenly –

SLAP! SLAP! SLAP! SLAP!

Footsteps behind me. As far as I know, worms – even *monster worms* – don't have feet.

I twist my head. I'm both very relieved and supremely annoyed to see that it's Quint.

'Quint!' I bark. 'I said split up. Why didn't you split?!'

'I did split!' he replies. 'When I split, I split left. That's how I split!'

'Splitting up isn't difficult, Quint!' I shout. 'Everyone just goes in different directions! That's the definition of "split up"! It's not rocket science!'

'Jack, I find rocket science easier to comprehend than your silly action plans!'

I yell at Quint, but he doesn't hear me. It's hard to hear anything over the sound of the worm slithering and slicing its way around the corner.

'Great job, Quint!' I holler. 'Because there are

two of us, the Wormungulous decided to follow us!'

There's a *KA-BAM* as the worm barrels through Foot Locker. The sound of shattering glass, twisting metal and bouncing Nikes echoes down the corridor.

It's time to try out my newest toy . . .

– The BOOMerang –
(a weapon that goes boom)

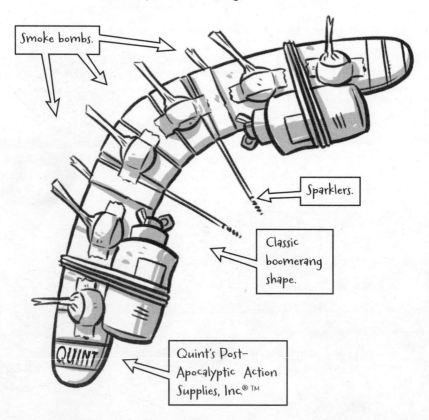

Smoke bombs.

Sparklers.

Classic boomerang shape.

Quint's Post-Apocalyptic Action Supplies, Inc.® ™

Quint, of course, is the designer of this particular gadget. It's supposed to 'distract and disorientate' monsters. I raise my hand, ready to throw, and –

chapter two

The BOOMerang does NOT come flying back
to me in the way it is supposed to – y'know, the
one quality that actually makes a boomerang
a *boomerang*. Without the 'coming back to you'
part, you're just flinging around curved wood –
not much fun.

The BOOMerang does not return, but it *does*
whack the Wormungulous in the face. There's a
BLAST as smoke bombs and sparklers explode.
The monster jerks to the left, veers back to the
right, and then –

ELEVATOR
SLAM!

I take that split second, when there's nothing but glass and metal in the air and wreckage in the worm's face, to grab Quint and yank him into the closest store. We tumble over a display table and crash to the floor.

'Stay down!' I whisper.

An instant later, the Wormungulous barrels down the corridor, streaking past the store like an oversized snot rocket come to life.

I catch my breath, get to my feet, and inch out into the corridor. The Wormungulous left a trail of yellow worm goo in its wake and the floor is now a slick mess. I watch the worm crash into a clothes store and disappear in a cloud of dust as the wall crumbles behind it.

'I didn't get a photo!' I exclaim.

'PHOTO FAIL,' Quint says.

I cock my eyebrow. 'Don't talk like that, Quint. It doesn't suit you.'

'A failure of photographic proportions, friend.'

'Better,' I say, slapping my best bud on the back. 'Now where are we?'

Looking around, I begin to tremble and shake as I realize: WE'RE INSIDE GAME!

'Dude!' I exclaim as I begin to walk the aisles. 'Could I have picked a better place for a last-minute hideout?'

'Quite perfect!' Quint exclaims happily.

Near the Nintendo 3DS section, I spot something I want so bad that it causes my gut to tighten up and my extremities to get all warm and tingly.

I'm staring at a giant, life-sized suit of space marine armour from my favourite game, NIMBUS: Call to Action. It's shiny, practically GLOWING.

There's a big sign next to it that says, 'Coming soon! The hottest sci-fi space marine first-person action shooter ever to hit the planet Earth! NIMBUS: Call to Action 14.'

Suddenly, I'm punched in the face by sadness. I'm thinking about how many amazing video games were being designed when the Monster Apocalypse happened. And now they'll never be released! I'll never get to play them!

I knock on the chest piece. *DONK DONK DONK*. It's definitely metal or some sort of fancy plastic.

Quint's eyes go wide. 'I was mistaken!' he exclaims. 'This silicone-plastic-Wonderflex is the finest in video game promotion!'

'I'm totally taking this,' I say. 'I'll be like an unstoppable space marine hero! I'll stuff some bottle rockets in the side here – any monsters get close and *VA-SHOOM!* Eat rocket!'

Quint grins. 'I must agree. It's quite impressive.'

'Now,' I say, 'where is our transportation?'

A moment later –

Rover! There you are, bud!

After about twenty clumsy attempts, Quint and I manage to get the space marine armour into Rover's saddle. Rover is my monster dog, and he can haul *anything*. I pocket a few PS4 games for the road, then step out into the gooey, slippery corridor.

'All right,' I say, 'let's find June and Dirk.'

chapter three

We're walking the upper level of the mall, looking down at the corridor below. I see all sorts of little kiosks that sell T-shirts and fancy cell phone cases and other crud that's really dumb but I also totally really kind of want. Most of the mall is a mess – looted and plundered by panicked people when the Monster Apocalypse first began.

Passing the Apple Store, I catch a whiff of something. A strange, sweet sort of odour, hanging in the air.

And I catch a flash of movement, below us. A figure, slinking around the corner, past Gap. An almost-human figure . . .

Seeing that – something *almost-but-not-quite* human – sends a chill of terror down my spine. My heart starts palpitating.

Maybe it was just a figment of my imagination . . .?

But no.

My eyes might play tricks on me, but not my nose. And the strange, sweet odour is growing stronger.

But it is not the odour of evil. It is not the foul stench that the villainous beast Blarg emitted. It is not the same stink that the Dozers and the Winged Wretches and other Wakefield monsters emanate. *That* is the smell of evil.

But this?

Honestly? It smells like a middle-school dance. It smells like, I realize, cheap aftershave.

'Quint, did you see that?' I whisper.

He nods. A huge helping of fear has appeared on his face. Fear with a side order of curiosity.

I pull my weapon, the Louisville Slicer, from its sheath.

It's been one month since we rescued June (sorta rescued) and we've still not seen a single other person. No kids, no adults, no nothing. Just zombies and monsters up the backside. And recently, even the zombies seem to be popping up less and less. In fact, it's like they're disappearing.

I mean, we've been at the mall over an hour now, and we haven't seen *one* zombie. And if you're a zombie expert like me, you know zombies are supposed to be, like, all over the mall. Ever see a zombie movie? Play a zombie video game? Zombies are ALWAYS at the mall. They just love shopping or something.

Quint believes something is *taking* the zombies. We haven't seen them migrating, and we haven't seen them just, like, dying off. I'll tell you this much: if something is taking the zombies, I do *not* want to meet whatever that 'something' is.

The sweet scent snaps my mind back to attention.

I drop to one knee and rub Rover behind the ears. 'Buddy, can you drag my space marine suit back to Big Mama?' I say, pointing in the direction of the parking lot, where Big Mama, our post-apocalyptic pickup truck, is waiting.

Rover tilts his head, then growls in understanding. A moment later he's trotting down the corridor, my space marine suit banging and clanging behind him.

'OK, Quint,' I say. 'Let's see what this thing is.'

Quint follows as I creep down the escalator to the main level. We duck behind a kiosk called Stuffed Stuff – it sells stuffed panda bears and piglets and ferrets. Holding my breath, I peek around the corner.

I see the figure again. And if it's a person, it's a *big* person. It's rattling one of the metal gates that hang over most of the storefronts.

Quint and I exchange terrified looks, then quietly sneak ahead to the next kiosk. We're like ultra-lame James Bonds. Do you think James Bond ever had to hide behind Cate's Custom Candles while trailing a target?

The strange figure comes to a stop in front of the Cinnabon bakery. I finally get a solid look at the thing. And what I see – it turns my blood to ice water.

I whip my head back around and drop to the floor. 'Did you see that?!' I ask Quint, trying to keep my voice to a whisper.

Quint nods. He doesn't speak. He's shaking like a leaf.

'It was like a monster-person. Or a person-monster,' I say. But before we can even begin to process the bonkers implications of that, a piercing shriek echoes down the hall.

It's June. She's rushing toward us. Dirk speeds alongside her. And behind them, colossal and charging with vicious fangs exposed, tearing through the mall like a train that's jumped the tracks, is the Wormungulous.

We need to find cover. Safety. Something to shield us from this beast.

But the giant metal gate that guards Sears department store looms ahead of us. Every store around us is gated. Locked tight.

We're in a dead end. Trapped.

No way out.

21

chapter four

I remember how I felt the instant before I defeated the big, bad, odorous, evil Blarg: terrified but confident. Frightened but *alive*.

That's how I feel now.

Brave.

Stupidly brave.

This is my moment.

The moment of Jack Sullivan, Post-Apocalyptic Action Hero.

The Wormungulous will be upon us in seconds. Its massive form is barrelling forward, turning everything in its path to dust. And I *can't* let my friends fall into the category of 'dust.' That's my biggest fear. That's what keeps me up at night (well, that and thoughts of Selena Gomez – I hope she's safe somewhere!).

I step toward the beast like some sort of samurai ninja Jedi.

'Jack, what are you doing?' June screams.

'June, Dirk, Quint. Get back,' I say. 'Behind me.'

'I'll try to open the gate into Sears,' Dirk says. 'If you can slow it down, maybe we won't all die today.'

I nod.

If Dirk gets that gate open, they can get to safety. But if not – they'll be squished, squashed, splattered. Done-zo.

'Jack . . .' June pleads.

'GO!' I shout. This feeling of samurai ninja Jedi heroism is totally beating out my feelings of butt-clenching fear, and I raise the dramatics up a notch.

June knows my goofiness. She knows I pretty much stumble and bumble my way through every monster encounter.

I blush. 'Sorry. Carried away. Just, please? Ah, *please*, go?'

KRAKA-SMASH!

The Wormungulous rips through the cell phone case kiosk. The walls quake. Glass falls and shatters from the railings above.

At last, June sprints toward Sears.

I stand tall. Blade at my side, like a cool, calm warrior. I can't take this ferocious, fanged beast head-on. But if I can do some nifty light-saber type moves, I might be able to buy my buds enough time to –

Jagged cracks spread through the floor like ice splintering on the surface of a pond. The Wormungulous's mouth opens, revealing a fat tongue darting around in the darkness of its gullet.

I take a deep breath.

And then, when the monstrous worm is nearly upon me, so close I can smell the rotten meat on its teeth, so close I can see my reflection in its hundred tiny eyes, I *leap* to the side. My fingers clench the blade, and I hold it with two hands, arms extended, parallel to the ground, gripping it as tight as I can as the worm blasts past me and the blade cuts into its flesh –

The monster shrieks in pain and its thick tail whips into me, and –

POW!

I slam into the side of the PacSun clothes store. I sag against the gate, then crash to the rubble-covered floor. Looking up, I see Dirk struggling to lift the heavy metal gate to Sears. Quint and June frantically help.

But it won't budge.

And it's too late.

The Wormungulous is upon them. The monster's mouth has closed and its wormy head is lowered, ploughing through the floor.

But then I see it.

The man-monster. He's rushing toward my friends. Quint spins around, horrified. The man-monster knocks him aside, grabs the gate, and lifts.

That's the last thing I see.

The worm's tail lashes me across the face, I'm flung to the floor, and everything goes black.

chapter five

I slowly blink my eyes open. I'm seeing stars
and spots and even four-leaf clovers – it's like a
whole Disney cartoon thing.

No sign of the others. I get to my feet and weave
my way toward Sears. The entire front of the store
has been destroyed.

I didn't stop the Wormungulous.

And my friends? Have I lost them?

Wreckage and debris litter the tiled floor. Water
rains down from the sprinkler system. Rubble from
the ceiling is scattered through the store.

What I spot next makes me go light-headed.

June's sneakers. The boy sneakers she wears that I love so much. One juts out from beneath a pile of wreckage.

No.

No, no, no.

My friends are buried beneath there. A pile of rubble as big as a February snowdrift.

I begin clawing and tearing at the debris. But it's all too big. Too heavy. My fingernail snaps as I struggle to lift the massive metal gate that blankets them.

My breath becomes ragged. I feel my eyes well up with tears.

And I smell – I smell –

I smell that pungent aftershave.

I spin around to see it. Gigantic and towering. The man-monster . . .

- The Man-Monster -

I don't draw my blade. I don't run. I just stand there. And then, still having said nothing, I turn around and continue trying to pry my friends free.

A warm hand grips the back of my neck. The man-monster's fingers close around my collar and I'm lifted into the air. He gently sets me down a few feet away.

The man-monster begins digging through the rubble, carefully pulling away huge chunks of ceiling. He removes bent and twisted pieces of gate. With one tremendous pull, he lifts the final piece away. And I see them.

My friends. Alive.

A little bloody, a lot dirty – but very much OK.

Relief floods through me. 'You're OK!'

June grins as she crawls from the pile and gets to her feet. *'You're* OK! Why did you just stand out there and try to stare the monster down? What is *wrong* with you?'

'I was trying to do a samurai thing.'

'No more samurai things, Jack.'

Quint stumbles from the rubble and throws his arms around me. My friends and I are not big huggers. But Quint squeezes me and slaps my back. 'I thought we were all done for!' he exclaims.

I smile. 'We're good, buddy. We're good.'

'Yes, we are,' June says, waving toward the man-monster. 'Thanks to *him*.'

Dirk nods. 'He punched through the gate. Pushed us inside. He took the brunt of the blow from the Wormungulous.'

So this . . . this man-monster, he not only freed my friends – he took the hit that saved their lives. And in a way, saved me – because without my friends, I might as well not exist.

This terrifying, wicked-looking thing is our saviour. Just goes to show – never judge a monster by its cover. Or its bone jewellery.

The creature suddenly gasps for breath and

drops to one knee. I see that his right leg is
injured. Probably battered while blocking my
friends. Pulling them free has taken everything
out of him.

The man-monster braces himself on a rack of
clothing and manages to stand again. And then
he opens his mouth.

The words practically knock me off my feet.
'You . . . you speak English?' I ask, stuttering.

'I speak more languages than you know,' the
man-monster says. His voice is a throaty growl.
He repeats, 'You are OK?'

'Yes,' I say. 'We are.'

'You are human?' the man-monster asks. He says 'human' like it's the first time he's ever spoken the word.

'Uh, yep,' I say, stepping forward. 'Sure am. Jack Sullivan is the name. And what are you?'

'Your tongue could not form the words,' the man-monster says.

'Oh. Well – do you have a name? A name that my, uh, lame, subpar tongue *could* form?'

'Thrull,' the man-monster says slowly.

'You saved us,' June says.

'Properly rescued our lives,' Quint chimes in.

'Real solid, monster bro,' Dirk adds. 'We owe you.'

Thrull is looking me up and down. His eyes focus on my shoulder. No – *over* my shoulder. The Louisville Slicer, in its sheath. He quickly reaches out and snatches it.

I take a very nervous step backward.

The Louisville Slicer is comically tiny in his big monster hands. His eyes narrow and he lifts the blade, gazing with focus.

'Your weapon . . .' he starts, his voice suddenly a notch softer.

'Yes. My weapon. And I'd love it back. But, uh, no rush. You're the boss here.'

His head tilts slightly to the side, causing the apparatuses and instruments around his neck to rattle and clang. 'This is the blade that felled the Œrṛūæl, the ancient evil, servant of Ṛeżżŏch the Ancient, Destructor of Worlds.'

'Uhhh . . . felled?' I ask.

'That means destroyed,' Quint whispers. 'As in: slain.'

'Oh. Oh yeah!' I exclaim. 'Yep! Well, I mean, it's my blade. I don't know who or what Œrṛūæl is. Or who he serves. Did you say Ṛeżżŏch the Ancient, Destructor of Worlds? Isn't he a Marvel villain? Or is that DC?'

The man-monster Thrull's eyes scrunch up and he looks at me like I'm slow. 'Marvel villain?'

Trying *not* to sound slow, I dive right back in. 'Oh yeah. Marvel. Um. Superheroes and stuff. They make all the best movies. Well, they did, when movies were still being made. But that's not important. So who is this Œrṛūæl? This thing that you think I, uh, "felled".'

Something like a smile appears on Thrull the man-monster's face. He hunches over and does a sort of impression, swinging his free arm.

'Blarg!' June suddenly exclaims. 'He means Blarg!'

Blarg is the titanic beast I defeated a month ago. He was crazy creepy and crazy evil – but now he's just crazy dead. 'Oh yeah, I felled him,' I say proudly. 'I *totally* felled him. But we didn't call him Œŕŗūæŀ, servant of Ŗeżżőcħ the Ancient, Destructor of Worlds, or whatever you said. We called him Blarg. 'Cause, ah, that's just the sound he made when he roared.'

I'm suddenly very embarrassed by our ability to creatively name monsters.

The man-monster Thrull takes three pained steps forward until he's fully towering over me. I'm afraid if I try to crane my neck any more, my head will pop off.

I gulp.

Was Blarg a friend of his? If so, he's probably pretty ticked about me slamming a blade into his buddy's brain. Should we be fleeing right now? I feel like maybe we should be fleeing . . .

But the next thing the man-monster Thrull does makes my jaw hang open . . .

'It takes a great hero to defeat a creature from the time before time,' Thrull says as he starts to stand up. 'To defeat a servant of Ŗeżżőch the Ancient, Destructor of Worlds.'

I timidly reach out and take the blade from him. 'Um. Well, thanks,' I say as I slip it back into the sheath. 'But it wasn't just me. I had my friends. This is Quint.'

Quint sticks out his hand. 'Pleased to meet you.'

'And June and Dirk,' I say.

They both wave awkwardly.

'So what are you doing here?' I ask.

'Here? Now? I am just trying to survive. But in my dimension? There, I was a monster hunter, like you.'

I feel myself blush. 'Monster hunter? Little old me? I'm not really a monster hunter,' I say.

'Wait,' Quint says. 'Do you know what *happened* here? On Earth?'

'Yeah!' June says, jumping in. 'You know what caused the Monster Apocalypse?'

Thrull's eyes narrow. 'Only pieces. But I know some, yes.'

Quint's giddy. 'We can finally learn, friends!' he says.

Suddenly, the man-monster Thrull drops to the floor. He moans in pain. His leg is worse off than I thought. 'My movement is limited. Help me?' Thrull says. 'To my friends? Home?'

I gulp. A monster home? Full of monster friends? 'Ah, where do you live?' I ask. 'Like a cave somewhere? Or an ancient castle? Or under a bridge?'

'ẞăġŋœ Ꝃðėn,' Thrull says. 'But I believe in your tongue, it is pronounced "Joe's Pizza".'

Quint and I look at each other, way beyond confused. And way beyond excited.

See, Joe's Pizza was an after-school hangout for middle-school kids, and an all-day hangout for older delinquent dudes, plus Dirk. On half days, kids would head there, grab a few slices, and generally cause mayhem.

Quint and I dreamed of being regulars there. Y'know, like on TV shows, how there are restaurants and hangouts where everyone *knows* you. Whenever you walk in, you'd just find your friends, chilling out. I imagined we'd just stroll in, everyone would wave, greet us, practically screaming our names – and our usual orders would be brought immediately.

But Quint and I were never invited to Joe's Pizza. And no way we were ever going to just show up and have all the other kids eyeing us and whispering, 'Who brought the dork squad?'

So yeah, it wasn't really our scene. I *wanted* it to be our scene. I would have given *anything* for it to be our scene. But it wasn't. Our scene was more 'stay at home, play Minecraft, let Quint's mom cook us Bagel Bites.'

Cool guys.

Def not cool guys.

But now . . .

Well?

Now it sounds like Joe's Pizza is an entirely different scene. A *monster* scene. And that causes Quint to begin rapidly hitting me . . .

Thrull looks up at me. I hand him my hockey stick (the one I conk zombie noggins with) to use as a crutch and we all help him to his feet.

'Yes,' I say. 'We'll get you back to Joe's Pizza.'

Dirk gathers up his gardening supplies. I sheath my weapon. Quint sniffs his armpit. And with that, our very strange group hobbles out of the Circle One Mall, home of the Wormungulous.

I have big plans for this mall – plans to *never* return.

chapter six

Thirty minutes later, the five of us – plus Rover
– are standing across the street from Joe's. And
my brain is just like, 'What the huh?!'

I see ample evidence that this is not the Joe's
Pizza we're used to . . .

– Ample Evidence –

Many-eyed monster.

Winged monster.

Oddly striking and dignified monster.

Lazy monster.

A bunch more monsters.

'Mr. Thrull, what exactly is this?' Quint asks.
'This is where I live,' he says, shifting and adjusting his weight on the hockey stick. 'Come.'

That sounds reasonable enough – but something stops me.

'Um, one second, Mr. Thrull!' I exclaim. 'Quick buddy huddle!'

I grab my friends and we all dash out of hearing distance.

'Should we go in there?' I ask.

Dirk and June both nod. 'I think so . . .' June says.

Of course! Why not?

'Why not?! You know how old folks always tell you not to trust strangers? Great advice! You know what's better advice? Don't trust *monster* strangers! *The dude's wearing bone jewellery.*'

Quint opens his mouth to respond, but a strange sound interrupts us. It's like the sound of a blade, slicing between us, silencing us.

'Do you guys hear that?'

It's like the wind, rustling through the trees. But louder. The sound fills the air. Like a flute or a, uh – what's that lame plastic instrument from elementary school? A recorder! It sounds a bit like that. But the sound is deeper, rougher – and the longer I listen to it, the more it begins to sound like a strange, devilish, musical scream. There's no other way to describe the sound. It is an inhuman SHRIEKING.

But there's no time to ponder the strange sound, because Thrull is limping toward Joe's. If we're going in, the time is now.

'Come on!' June says.

I listen to the noise a moment longer. The sound enters my ears and proceeds to march straight down my spine, twisting it, terrifying me to my core.

It's only a noise.

Yet it scares me beyond belief.

'Jack!' Quint barks. I shake my head, trying to shake out the fear, and I reluctantly follow my friends. From inside Joe's, I hear glass shatter and freakish, inhuman laughing.

But I continue following.

We all do.

Rover trots beside me. As we step up onto the sidewalk, I tell him to stay, and he flashes those puppy-dog eyes at me. 'Don't worry. We'll be back, buddy,' I say. 'I think . . .'

Continuing forward, we pass the monsters hanging out outside. I try to give them good, solid, manly nods – but they just look at me like, 'Buddy, you are in the *wrong* place.'

Thrull places his hand against the door, and pushes it open, and we step inside. Inside, to the strangest sight imaginable . . .

Tentacles dance in the air! Furry beasts arm-wrestle! Scaled things play some strange version of darts. At the counter, insect-like monsters suck down entire pizzas in a single bite. Small flying creatures swoop through the air, delivering food. And everywhere, at tables, in booths, are HULKING MONSTERS chatting it up in some sort of monster language.

A few speak English. Bits and pieces of
strange monster dialogue float over:

'. . . ONCE POUNDED A GURLAK INTO THE
MUD WITH JUST MY TAIL . . .'

'. . . MORE SNOZZLE STEAKS, CHEF! . . .'

'. . . TASTES BETTER WHEN IT'S STILL
BREATHING, IF YOU ASK ME . . .'

49

A massively round monster behind the bar
wings a pizza pie through the air, directly
into the mouth of a heaving creature that is
seemingly all mouth and nothing else.

And then there's us.

There's me.

The thirteen-year-old human.

The scared, confused, overconfident-but-
only-overconfident-in-order-to-hide-his-
crippling-fear kid.

'My friends!' Thrull bellows. 'Listen!'

The grumble of monster voices grows quiet. They turn in their chairs. Some crane impossibly long necks. I can feel their eyes – some with thousands of little eyeballs, like flies – watching us.

MEET JACK, AND HIS FRIENDS. THESE HUMANS BESTED THE ANCIENT ONE, ŒRŖŪÆŁ!

Um, we call him Blarg. Remember?

Thrull purses his lips. He sighs through his neck-gills, then says, 'Œŗŗūæl, known in this world as BLARG!'

The monsters simply stare. Silence hangs in the air like a poorly timed fart. Finally, a small, zero-armed creature, perched on a chair, laughs and leans forward. 'This small human defeated a servant of Ṛeżżőch the Ancient, Destructor of Worlds? HA! Not likely!' the creature says, cackling.

Hey! Are they calling me a liar?! I'm many things. I'm lazy. I'm clumsy. I'm a sucker for girls with British accents. I'm pretend-charming but not real-charming. But I'm no liar.

Well, that's not totally true, either. I mean, I've lied plenty. Who hasn't?

But I'm not lying about this!

I cough into my fist, take a deep breath, and step forward. 'Um. Ah. No. It's true. I did. For real. With this,' I say as I pull the Louisville Slicer from its sheath.

The way the monsters react, you'd think I'd just pulled a severed donkey head from my back pocket. Some gasp like humans. Others make sounds that I can only assume are monster versions of gasps.

They begin to sniff the air and then start to smile. It's like they can smell Blarg on the blade.

Thrull looks at me with a grin that's all teeth.

He rests one massive paw on my shoulder. I can't help but feel all warm inside . . .

And then –

'And these are my friends!' I say, shouting to be heard over the roar. 'I didn't do it alone! They helped! Like, a whole bunch!'

The crowd cheers louder. June and Quint beam. Dirk gives me a slap on the back. And that is how we're welcomed into the strange new world of Joe's Pizza.

Soon, monsters are surrounding us, asking questions, telling stories, offering us food. A dozen monsters crowd around me as I recount the tale of how I battled Blarg. They keep pouring me flat Joe's soda and I keep talking.

Later on, I spot Thrull, off in a dim corner, sitting at a table. He's talking with another creature – this one thin, with spindly limbs and a rough, jagged beard.

Thrull catches my eye and beckons me over. I pull Quint, Dirk, and June with me.

'Please sit,' Thrull says, then indicates the other monster. 'This is ßàr̠g̠tʻ – pronounced "Bardle" in your tongue.'

Bardle smiles – an act that seems to take him great effort. His face scrunches up, revealing deep scars slashing this way and that.

'Bardle is aged,' Thrull says. 'For many lifetimes, he was a conjurer in our dimension.'

'Dimension?' Quint asks, leaning forward.

PLEASE SIT.
I WILL TELL YOU WHAT
I KNOW. WHAT I KNOW
OF HOW WE CAME TO
BE HERE . . .

chapter seven

IN OUR DIMENSION, THERE WAS A LEGEND. A STORY, TOLD TO KEEP YOUNG ONES AWAKE AT NIGHT. THE STORY OF A BEING KNOWN AS ṚEŻŻÓCḤ THE ANCIENT, DESTRUCTOR OF WORLDS.

'How ancient is he? Older than you?' June asks.

Bardle chuckles. 'Oh yes. Much. Ṛeżżócḥ the Ancient comes from the time before time, when great battles were fought in our lands. After an age, Ṛeżżócḥ was defeated. And for millennia, he was gone. We lived in peace.

'But he returned. Throughout the ages, there have been rare, evil creatures who strive to bring about the return of Ṛeżżőch. One of these servants of Ṛeżżőch awakened his spirit. And Ṛeżżőch came like a summer storm, hard and fast, wielding magic more powerful than we had ever known. In his sleep, his hunger had grown strong.'

'I know the feeling,' I say. 'Sometimes when I wake up, I'm just craving a Mars Bar, like –'

'Jack!' Quint whispers.

'Oh. Right. Story time.'

Bardle chuckles. 'Ṛeżżőch did not crave "Mars Bars". Ṛeżżőch craved death. He is the destructor.'

I gulp. That sounds bad.

'Ṛeżżőch's magic had grown strong,' Bardle continues. 'And then, at the peak of his power – *it happened*. In an instant, our world turned dark. The skies clouded. The atmosphere crackled. Doors opened – portals of energy. I do not know how. I do not know if it was Ṛeżżőch himself who opened the doors – or something else . . .'

Quint shoots me a nervous look. None of this is sounding good.

Bardle continues, 'But I know that next, we were *sucked* through those doors. All of us: the wild vines, the undead who carry and spread the zombie plague, my friends whom you see here – all of us, in an instant, propelled through a thousand doors, into your world.'

'Wait,' I say. 'And then this bad guy, Rężżőcħ the Ancient – he came through these energy door portal gate things? HE'S HERE?!'

Bardle shakes his head. 'No. The doors closed before Rężżőcħ could come through. Rężżőcħ the Ancient was left behind. For us, it is a relief – we suffered under his rule. But now we are here, in a new, strange world.'

'Oh,' I say softly. 'But, so – are we safe from this Ṛeżżőcħ fella?'

Bardle nods. 'It seems that way. For now. He was left behind in our world. We are now in yours.'

Phew.

Bardle smiles. 'And we owe you a great deal of thanks for defeating Blarg. He was a servant of Ṛeżżőcħ. One who worshipped him. One who would do his best to bring Ṛeżżőcħ into this world.'

Thrull takes a break from chomping on something that looks like fried rat tail. 'You are building a bestiary?' he grunts.

'How did you know?' I ask.

'I see your friend writing and writing. And you have a device for image capture, correct?'

I look down to the camera around my neck. Before the Monster Apocalypse, I took photos for the school paper. I wasn't half-bad, either. Photography is kinda my thing – photography and monster-slaying. 'Yes,' I say.

'May I see this bestiary?' Thrull asks. Bardle cocks a sharp eyebrow at Thrull, but Quint shrugs and hands over his notebook.

I watch as Thrull feels the weight of it in his massive hands. He opens it up and examines

the three-ring binder like an infant touching
something for the first time. At last, he shakes
his head and says, 'No, no – this won't do at all.'

Quint and I frown. He's bad-mouthing our
bestiary?

Thrull reaches into one of the bags draped
over his shoulder and removes a thick, dusty
tome. He holds it out.

As I reach for this new book, I feel something
like energy leap into my fingertips. My hands
are tingly. Sound seems to fade, like someone
is turning down the volume. My breaths come
short and quick.

My hand trembles as I lift open the heavy
cover.

And immediately sneeze.

'Uh, sorry,' I say, feeling really doofy.

No one says anything. My friends stare,
eyes wide, at the book. The cover is made of
something hard, like old monster skin. The
pages are yellow and thick and textured. Each
one is covered with creepy sketches of strange,
terrifying creatures. Words scrawled in monster
writing.

And *stuff*.
Things.

Teeth and fingernails and hair and – *eww* – a flattened eyeball.

'Um . . . what is this disgusting but awesome book?' I ask.

Thrull grins proudly. 'THAT is a bestiary. A true bestiary. From our world.'

Bardle looks at Thrull. I sense anger from Bardle, though I don't know why.

I continue flipping through the pages. Every page past the twentieth or so is blank. No entries.

I look up, confused.

'It is a gift,' Thrull says. 'For defeating Blarg, Servant of Ŗeżżóch. For helping me back to my home. It is an unfinished bestiary. Much better than your flimsy notebook. Two hundred and thirty-two blank pages. They are yours to fill.'

I look to Quint. He's practically giddy. 'I don't know what to say . . .'

'Hold up . . . Do you expect us to go around, like, plucking monsters' eyeballs out?' June asks. ''Cause we're not really eyeball pluckers.'

Thrull erupts with laughter. I guess he gets a kick out of eyeball-plucking imagery. 'No, no,' he says at last. 'But if you want to be makers of a bestiary, you should capture the "essence" of each creature. Proof. A single hair. A drop of sweat. A bestiary scholar who does not, in fact, *encounter* the monster – in our dimension he might be described as, well, a coward.'

'We're no cowards,' Dirk says.

Thrull chuckles. 'I thought not.'

Bardle remains silent. He seems to watch the whole conversation suspiciously. I feel less than welcome.

Suddenly, June yanks my camera over my head and exclaims, 'Photo time! Everyone say *monster apocalypse!'*

It's past midnight when we finally excuse ourselves and head home, promising to return soon.

As we walk out, I look to Quint, grinning. 'We've got a *real-deal* bestiary now. We're going to search high and low for strange creatures. This is the *best quest ever!'*

chapter eight

We all agree: we've seen our friends turned to zombies, we've seen giant monsters devour those zombies, we've seen Quint without pants – but *today* was the strangest day of our lives.

A few blocks from Joe's, Quint stops. He pulls the bestiary from his bag and sets it on the bonnet of a banged-up Wakefield police cruiser. He pulls a pen from his pocket and starts writing.

'Whatcha doing, buddy?' I ask.

'I'm adding our first entry to the new bestiary. The Wormungulous.'

'But we don't have its "essence". You know, proof, like Thrull said.'

Quint smiles slyly. 'Yes, we do. Hand me the Louisville Slicer.'

I unsheathe the blade. Quint holds it up, turning and examining it in the moonlight. Finally, he seems satisfied. Gripping the blade in one hand and holding the bestiary with the other, Quint wipes the edge of the bat on the page.

We all inch closer. A gob of almost-dried Wormungulous blood and gunk rubs off. Quint writes for a few moments, then looks up proudly. 'One down, two hundred and thirty-one to go . . .'

THE WORMUNGULOUS
(Ingens Vermis)

DATA (Quint's best approximations):
Length: 90 feet
Weight: 30–35 tons
Speed: 40 mph on surface;
subterranean speed currently unknown

Spiky
tentacles.

ESSENCE:
Wormungulous blood.

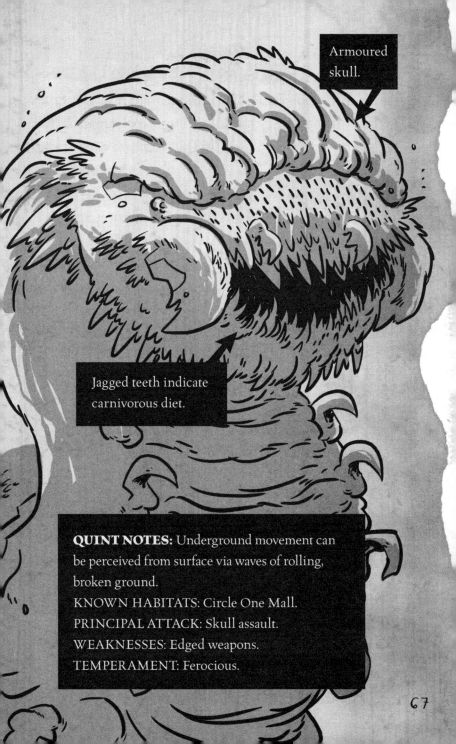

Armoured skull.

Jagged teeth indicate carnivorous diet.

QUINT NOTES: Underground movement can be perceived from surface via waves of rolling, broken ground.
KNOWN HABITATS: Circle One Mall.
PRINCIPAL ATTACK: Skull assault.
WEAKNESSES: Edged weapons.
TEMPERAMENT: Ferocious.

Nearing our tree house, I smile. We're home. Feels good to be home after *the weirdest day ever*.

And what a home it is. See, I was an orphan before the Monster Apocalypse. My foster family, the Robinsons, were real jerks. But they built their kid – my foster brother – a *ridic* tree house. The Robinsons hightailed it as soon as the Monster Apocalypse hit – I have no idea

Catapult #1.

Zip line (great for last-minute escapes—also for drying socks).

Mountain Dew distillery (working on perfecting the formula—currently just hot dog water and green food coloring).

Toilet bucket.

where they are now. But that's fine: Quint and I moved into the tree house and spent a lot of time tricking it out. It is *serious*.

Crow's nest (with night-vision telescope).

Bottle-rocket launchers.

Heli-pad for RC helicopter.

Catapult #2.

Crossbow.

Rainwater shower.

Weatherproof flat-screen TV.

Relaxation Station (video games and comic books and RISK).

Electric generator.

Armoury.

Outer defences (sharp!).

Quint places the bestiary in our reinforced snack lockbox. It's where we keep all our most valuable possessions: Twinkies, burp-contest scorecard (no one ever beats June), my spare nunchucks – all the good stuff.

Quint locks it, and my friends head to bed.

But I don't doze off.

I worry.

I spent a lifetime – well, like thirteen years; actually less, 'cause for a while I was a baby and then a toddler and y'know – but I've spent a LONG time wanting buddies. A *family*.

And now that I've got it – I'm scared to total extreme death of losing that family.

With everything quiet, I replay the day's events in my head. One image haunts me.

Not Joe's Pizza.

Not the image of Wormungulous.

It's the Wormungulous slamming into my friends. It's that feeling in my stomach when I thought they were gone for good. It won't go away.

I can't shake it.

After two hours of kicking and turning and tossing (is there anything worse than trying to go to sleep and not being able to?), I finally give up.

I climb out of bed, squinting in the darkness, and shuffle out to the deck.

Rover scampers over and wiggles into the pulley basket. I flip the hydraulic lift switch, and his huge hide is hoisted up onto the deck.

I fix us some cocktails – I like Coke mixed with Dr Pepper, and Rover is a fan of Fanta Orange and grass, topped with acorns. I pour some into his monster food bowl, which is actually a hollowed-out Dozer skull. Rover slurps from the eyeball socket.

I kick back and stare out at the moonlit destruction. The world is changing. Strange vines crawl up and over everything. The decomposing body of the monster Blarg is still draped across my foster parents' house. His evil odour hangs in the air. The monsters at Joe's Pizza, though – they don't have that smell. They just generally smell like a gym locker.

I knock back half the soda in one gulp. I anxiously tap the bottle against my knee. 'Can I tell you a secret, Rover?'

'Purr.'

'I wasn't scared before. Not like this. At the mall, watching all my friends almost get crushed by that worm, I was petrified. If it wasn't for Thrull, they'd be gone. Dead.'

'Purrr.'

'I'm Jack Sullivan, Post-Apocalyptic Action Hero. But they're not.'

'Purrr.'

I sigh. 'I wish I could just, I don't know, just like, lock everyone up in this tree house so no one could ever, ever leave, no matter what.'

Yep . . . yep. I heard it as soon as I said it. That was creeper-ish.

Rover lowers his head and places his jaw on the back of his paws. It's impossibly cute. I think he does that when he knows I'm a stressed mess.

'I just . . . I don't know. It's like I'm supposed to protect these people now. But what do I know about that? Nothing except for nothing!'

'You know a lot,' a voice says.

I practically jump out of my skin and whirl around. It's Quint. He's in his mad-scientist bathrobe. That's right – Quint has a bathrobe that looks like a lab coat. He actually owns that.

'Sorry, friend,' he says. 'Did I scare you?'

'Yes,' I say. 'Drink?'

Quint shrugs and takes a swig. He plops down on the seat beside me. 'I couldn't sleep, either.'

'Oh,' I say, softly.

'You know, you're not alone, Jack,' he says. 'We're *all* Post-Apocalyptic Action Heroes now.'

I sigh. 'I know, but it's just, I don't want to – '

'Lose anyone else?' Quint asks. 'We all feel the same way.'

We sit in silence. I hear crickets chirping – a nice reminder that not *everything* from our old world is gone.

But then I hear something else.

That same strange, whistling scream that we heard outside of Joe's Pizza. As I've dubbed it in my head: The Shrieking.

The longer we listen, the louder it seems to grow. The sound is bouncing around inside my skull like a pinball.

Standing up, I glimpse a pair of zombies – the first zombies we've seen all day, weirdly – shuffling down the middle of the street. They disappear behind a house, then reappear a minute later. Their heads are raised, like they're moving with purpose. This isn't the usual mindless bumbling about.

'Something's up,' I say as I race up the spiral ladder to the telescope and peer through it.

I dash back down the steps, leaving the telescope spinning. 'This could be what's causing them to disappear! Like, they're going somewhere – and not coming back . . .'

A smile begins to spread across Quint's face. He's intrigued. His science noggin is science nogginning. 'We must investigate!' he says.

I stop.

This is my biggest fear.

This is why I couldn't sleep.

Quint, wanting to do something daring and adventurous – something daring and adventurous that could get him totally devoured and leave him, like, headless. Headless Quint. That's my nightmare.

It's no big deal, Jack. Relax.

'It *is* a big deal!' I exclaim.

'Huh?' Quint says.

'Oh. Never mind. Sorry. Look, it's just – it's just too dangerous to go out there.'

'Pardon?' Quint says. 'I've been wondering about the disappearing zombies for *weeks*. I knew something was afoot. And now it's clear: something truly *is* afoot – and we're not going to go seek the source?!'

'No. *I* am. You're not.'

Quint gives me a long, pained look. His mouth hangs open, just slightly. 'Excuse me?' he finally says. His voice sounds choked.

'I'm going alone.'

Quint steps toward me, suddenly standing stiff and straight. 'Like fun you are. Either we both go, or neither of us goes.'

'I can't keep risking my friends all willy-nilly!' I exclaim. 'I also can't keep saying things like "willy-nilly"! And you're causing me to do both!'

Suddenly, The Shrieking spikes – a sharp howl
that slices through the night air like a knife.
We both snap our heads in the direction of the
chilling sound.

We *need* to know what's happening. And I
know – I KNOW – Quint won't let me go without
him.

'Fine,' I say at last. 'Get dressed.'

'I am dressed.'

I eye his silly lab-coat bathrobe. 'Really?
That's all you're gonna wear?'

Quint nods. 'Come, Jack. Let's make haste.'

'Making haste in bathrobes,' I mutter. 'Ridiculous . . .'

I grab the Louisville Slicer and slide down the fire escape pole. Quint and Rover follow in the pulley basket, and then we mount up. Me in the saddle, Quint in the rear, setting off into the cool, misty night.

chapter nine

Without streetlamps or cities to light the sky, it's impossibly dark. Trees, unattended and overgrown, loom over us like shadowy figures. But as we ride, the clouds shift, the moon shines bright, and the sky seems extra huge. The stars look so big they could blind you.

Rover quietly carries us down a winding road. Houses have begun to crumble as the Vine-Thingies choke them.

Up ahead, zombies shuffle across the road, following the sound.

'It's like the Pied Piper of Hamelin,' Quint whispers. 'He was a dude who played a flute that lured rats to their death. The rats just followed the sound. They couldn't help it.'

'That happened?' I say. 'When? Like, back in the nineties?'

'No, Jack. It's a myth from the sixteenth century.'

'Oh.'

As we near Main Street, the crowd of shuffling zombies grows thicker. Oddly, they take no interest in our fleshy bodies. They are focused on only one thing: The Shrieking.

I feel Quint's fingers tighten around my jacket. 'Um, Jack. Could we find a more – uh – secure place to figure out what's going on?'

'Good call,' I say. 'Higher ground. We can see how big this zombie parade really is.'

I tug on Rover's reins, steering him down a cramped alley. Ahead of us looms the Old South Graveyard.

'Jack – really?' Quint groans. 'Things aren't creepy *enough* with the zombies and the whistling? You're taking us into the town *graveyard?*'

'There,' I say, pointing to a giant tomb atop the hill at the centre of the cemetery. 'We'll be able to see most of Wakefield from there.'

With barely a running start, Rover bounds over the cracked stone wall and we land inside the cemetery. Rover makes his way up the sloping hill. Then he springs forward, and we land atop the tomb. And from there, we see it all. Zombies as far as the eye can see . . .

'It is *definitely* a Pied-Piper sort of thing,' Quint says. 'There must be *thousands*.'

I raise my camera to snap a photo but suddenly feel Quint's fingers digging into my neck. I spin around. Quint looks like he's about to cry. Or vomit. Or both. At the same time. Which is just a really weird, awful image.

'What is it?' I ask, but then I feel it, too. A quaking at my feet. A rumbling from inside the tomb. I look down. The stone beneath us is beginning to crack.

'Quint,' I say softly, my skin beginning to crawl with fear. 'Let's go home. Now. Both of us.'

But it's too late –

I'm flung through the air like a rag doll. Quint smacks into a headstone. Rover hits the grass, flips, and tumbles down the hill.

'Quint, duck!' I shout as chunks of stone and concrete rain down. The rubble pounds the grass like a meteor shower. It's like the tomb was detonated from the inside out. Like something suddenly ripped through it . . .

Woozy, gripping the damp dirt, I get to my knees. And what I see makes my blood run ice cold . . .

- THE HAIRY EYEBALL MONSTER! -

Ridonc size.

Single, solitary, super-scary eyeball.

Could really use a haircut.

The long fur on the monster's back straightens and stands up on end. The hair is no longer just hair – it's a million silvery, spiny quills.

I quickly snap a photo. The flash explodes like white phosphorus in the darkness. The eyeball's iris splits open with a nauseating *SHLUCK* sound and the beast emits an earsplitting roar. The open iris reveals nothing but red and blue pulp – like the insides of some strange, nightmarish fruit.

'Jack!' Quint exclaims. 'I don't believe it likes being photographed!'

'But it's for the bestiary!'

The tremendous eyeball rolls forward. Its needle-like quills puncture the earth. Soon, a vast array of razor-sharp quills is aimed at us, like an army of medieval spears.

'It's going to run us over! Pincushion style!' I say, spinning on my heels. 'C'mon!'

Quint dashes ahead of me and together we race down the hill.

KRAK! KRUNCH! SMASH!

The sound of shattering headstones explodes behind us as the Hairy Eyeball Monster thunders after us.

'Faster, Quint!'

Quint doesn't need to be told twice. He runs headlong – *too* headlong. He pitches forward, screeches, then slams into a headstone with an unquestionably painful *KRAK*.

And suddenly, *FLIT!*

A high-pitched whistle – and one of the Hairy Eyeball Monster's quills blasts past me, nearly piercing my ear. The monster fired it like a rocket!

Quint cries out.

My legs go weak.

I see the quill. It's jutting through Quint's back, penetrating my friend. Quint's eyes are shut tight. His body is slumped in the dirt, limp, pinned to the headstone.

chapter ten

His face is pale and there are dark circles beneath his eyes. 'It's been fun, friend,' he says. He coughs twice. 'Tell the world – tell the world our story . . .'

There's an aching in the back of my throat. My stomach rolls as I look down at the injury, expecting to see something bloody and awful: a razor-sharp quill slicing through my best friend.

But I see none of that.

Tears – real tears! – well up behind my eyeballs.

I sigh. 'I know you want to do a dramatic Hollywood goodbye. But dude, you're one hundred percent *fine!* Your bathrobe is just pinned to the headstone.'

'Wait, for real, I'm OK?'

'Yes!' I say, grabbing hold of the needle. I start to tug but immediately yank my hand away. It's razor sharp.

The ground shakes as the Hairy Eyeball Monster hurtles down the hill.

'Quint, quick, out of the bathrobe!' I say.

'I'll be naked!' he exclaims.

'You'll have your boxers! And your T-shirt!'

'But I'll be chilly!' he cries.

The roar of the barrelling monster grows closer.

'Chilly or dead, Quint,' I bark. 'Your choice!'

Quint mutters something. He tries to get one arm out of the robe, but he ends up sort of looping it around himself. In seconds, he's completely upside down, stuck even more than before, and he's managed to turn his goofy bathrobe into what appears to be a makeshift straitjacket.

This could be going better.

Every few moments a *KRASH* rings out as another headstone bursts and the Hairy Eyeball closes in. 'Quint!' I yell, finally just grabbing hold of him and tugging. 'Are you trying to get us killed?'

He is so tangled in the bathrobe that the whole thing just ends up getting sliced to pieces as I

yank him to his feet. He sprints down the hill
and I follow.

I crane my neck. The eyeball begins to tremble
and shake – and I realize, with *supreme terror*,
that we're about to wind up on the wrong end of
a barrage of ten thousand needles.

'Quint! Cover! Now!'

We slip behind the two nearest headstones.
And just in time –

FLIT! FLIT! FLIT!

NEEDLE ATTACK!

Needles pepper our little tombstone defences. The cement cracks and breaks and crumbles. I feel like I'm in some video game with the world's most poorly designed cover system. Like, not Uncharted. Something cruddy.

'What do we do?' Quint hollers.

'Um, off the top of my head? Maybe, y'know, LEAVE! AS SOON AS IT STOPS SHOOTING!'

'But the zombie parade!' Quint cries. 'I must know more!'

'Quint, I'm not dying in a cemetery! It's too fitting! Too perfect!'

'Fine,' Quint says. 'But if it *is* a Pied-Piper thing, The Shrieking will occur again. And next time, we *will* track down the source.'

'Sure, fine, deal!' I shout. 'Assuming we get out of here alive!'

Finally, the barrage of needles stops. I peek around the side. My tombstone cover is cracked and the stone is filled with needles.

The Hairy Eyeball Monster is bald now. Its needles have all been launched. It reminds me of one of those creepy, hairless cats – but instead of skin, it's made of, like, eyeball covering. It's like . . . the *Hairless* Eyeball Monster.

The monster's skin bulges – and there's a sick

tearing sound as thick, dark needles begin to protrude from it once again. The beast howls in what I can only guess is pain as the quills begin to pop and poke through its membrane-y hide.

'It's reloading!' I say as I pop up and grab Quint. 'Now's our chance!'

We half-run, half-stumble down the long, headstone-dotted hill. At the bottom, Rover is waiting for us, tongue out, big tail wagging. Quint and I scramble up onto his back.

'Rover, go!' I shout.

With a single leap, we're out of the cemetery. The enraged roar of the Hairy Eyeball Monster cuts through the quiet of the night.

chapter eleven

When I wake the next morning, I'm sore all over. I have aches and pains in places that I didn't even know were capable of producing aches and pains.

It takes me a moment to remember *why* I feel like the last man standing in the Royal Rumble.

Oh yeah . . . Last night.

With the immediate danger of the Hairy Eyeball Monster over, my mind goes to the zombie parade and The Shrieking. That's the scariest thing yet; scary because it felt like something was controlling the zombies. Some sound drawing them in. Some great, evil force at work.

My eyes flicker open and suddenly it's *me* doing the shrieking. Dirk and June are staring at me like I'm some sort of alien who just landed on Earth.

I sit up and wipe drool from my lip. A big patch of saliva shaped like Darth Vader has formed on my pillow. I awkwardly try to prop my elbow over it. Don't need June seeing my Darth Vader drool.

'Would you guys believe me if I said we went to a parade?' I ask.

Dirk throws one boot-clad foot up on the table and sips from a mug of hot coffee. 'No, I would not.'

'Well, take a look at this,' I say, grabbing my camera and tossing it to June. June glances down and her eyes go wide. I'm waiting for her to gasp, exclaim, or express shock somehow – but instead she just bursts out laughing.

'Stop, stop, wait!' I say, scrambling out of my little sleep area and yanking the camera from June's hands. I frantically flip past the beyond-embarrassing photos. 'Here, this one. Don't click backward. Just forward. *Just. Forward.*'

June, still giggling, clicks ahead – and her giggling quickly comes to a halt. Her eyes are wide as she looks at the endless march of zombies. 'There are so many of them . . .' she says softly.

'We could have wiped a whole load of them out at once,' Dirk growls. 'Should have brought me with you.'

'Dirk, we don't wipe out zombies. Zombies used to be people. We only wipe out the bad monsters. Anyway, you can't tell from the photo, but the zombies were all marching together – like they were going somewhere. Quint can probably explain better . . .'

June hands me back the camera. 'Quint's in his workshop.'

Dirk nods. 'I heard three explosions, two bangs, and a bunch of "gee-golly-willikers". Kid must be working on something real nuts.'

I'm not surprised. After what we saw last night, I'm sure Quint's got ideas for about six new gadgets and nineteen possible plans of attack.

'Guys,' I say after a moment. 'We heard that

shrieking noise again. It was like *that noise* was calling the zombies, making them go toward it.'

June and Dirk exchange worried glances. 'Well . . . where did they go?'

'Don't know. We only followed them as far as Main Street. That's when we ran into the Hairy Eyeball Monster.'

'Excuse me? The what?' June asks.

I plop my head back down in the Darth Vader drool and wave at the camera. 'Next pic.'

June clicks and her eyes almost pop out of her skull. Dirk leans over, looks at the picture, and cracks his knuckles.

'Yeah,' I say. 'The situation got a little . . . hairy.'

I grin. Dirk and June look at me like I'm quite dumb.

'That's a great joke! Situation got *hairy*! A monster that's all *hair*? C'mon!'

Still no one laughs. June shakes her head. 'Jack, you shouldn't have gone without us. We're a team, remember?'

I shrug. 'You were sleeping.'

June looks like she's about to slug me.
But I'm saved . . . Saved by Quint.

He's in the yard, shouting, 'Friends! Hurry
down here, please. I have something to unveil!'

chapter twelve

> Jack, if you would, please walk toward me.

> I don't like this. Not one bit.

June elbows me. 'Aww, what's the matter, Jack? Scared to cross your own backyard?'

'Me? Scared? Ha!' I say. I boldly stomp toward Quint. Grass squishes loudly beneath my sneakers.

This is no problem.

ZERO problem.

But Quint grins then. A sick grin. A devious

Quint grin. Devious Quint grins are never good. The kid looks like a Bond villain every time he plots a move in Monopoly.

My next step is followed by a sudden snapping sound as something tightens around my ankle. It's like a hand, snatching me. 'ZOMBIE IN THE GROUND!!!!' I shriek. 'GROUNDERS! WE GOT GROUNDERS!'

And then –

OK.
False alarm.
Not grounders.

Please just forget that ever happened – me, yelling about grounders. Grounders aren't a thing.

It was, in fact, a Quint invention.

A particularly cruel Quint invention.

June bursts out laughing – she has a deep, loud laugh that makes my heart happy – and Dirk chuckles like a little kid.

Quint talks to Dirk and June like he's Iron Man presenting some new suit of armour.

'Now,' Quint says, 'I assume you're wondering why our friend Jack is hanging upside down?'

'Not really,' Dirk says.

'I'm just enjoying it,' June says. 'He'd make a good Christmas tree ornament. Just wrap some lights around him. What do you say, Jack?'

'I hate all of you,' I mutter.

'That's not very festive,' June says.

'Listen carefully,' Quint says. 'I've long suspected zombies were disappearing. Two months ago, we couldn't turn a corner without a zombie pouncing. Now, zombie hidey-holes are nearly empty! I didn't know *why* until last night, when we heard The Shrieking and saw the parade –'

'Um, guys,' I interrupt. 'All the blood is rushing to my head. I can't really see . . .'

My friends ignore me. Of course. 'You're telling me some – ah – some *thing* is making a freaky shrieking sound – and that sound is calling zombies away from Wakefield?' Dirk asks.

'But what?' June asks.

'I don't know,' Quint says. 'In fact, I haven't the faintest idea.'

June gives me another little shove. 'Can I just again mention how much I absolutely love upside-down Jack?' she says. 'Can we keep him like this?'

Finally, I erupt. 'FIRST! Everyone stop pushing me. SECOND! What does me hanging here have to do with all this? Why did I get snared?'

'Because,' Quint says, 'we're going to use a snare to catch our very own zombie. We'll bring the zombie here. And then . . .'

The next time we hear The Shrieking, we set the zombie loose. And we follow it. That's how we solve this mystery . . .

chapter thirteen

Moments before I go unconscious, June and Dirk let me down from the zombie snare. Some pals, huh?

I'm still filthy from last night's battle, so I use our rainwater shower to freshen up. In the shower, chewing on my muddy nails, I noodle our situation.

And I don't like it . . .

Discovering a pizza place full of monsters? That's heavy! Learning that the Earth is now covered in monsters from, like, a time before time began to tell time? Also super heavy.

And that's just like the weirdness appetizer! The main course is what appears to be the *real threat*: some strange, eerie sound – The Shrieking – that causes zombies to lose what little minds they have left.

Where could they be going?

After my shower, I stick my head into Quint's workshop. I spot ropes and wires and hooks. 'Quint, buddy, how much time do you need to create these zombie traps?'

'Two days,' he says. 'Three days tops.'

My insides are being twisted by fear. This is

a great big problem. And I only know one way to deal with great big problems . . .

AVOID THEM!

So with two days (three days tops) until we can tackle The Shrieking, I decide to throw myself headlong into Action Jack Bestiary Questing Mode.

I can picture us showing Thrull the finished book, dusty and old and from another land. Proof of the completed quest. Proof that I'm a fantastic, monster-documenting photojournalist. I want that proof!

June's helping Dirk tend to his little vegetable garden when I stroll over. Dirk's whining about weeds and chewing on a carrot like Bugs Bunny.

'Guys,' I say. 'Quint needs two days to build his zombie traps. So while we're waiting . . .'

Let's quest.

We start at home and work outward. Bestiary building is a very systematic process. You must search beneath rocks, inside abandoned old cars – *everywhere*.

The first day, we catalogue six different creatures.

The next morning, I'm up early – before the sun's risen. I pop in on Quint. He's still working on his traps. He does it by candlelight, and he looks like some creepy old innkeeper.

After a breakfast of grilled crab apples and stale Pop-Tarts, we head out, on the hunt.

We've just finished scooping up some essence from this nasty Sludge Savage –

When we hear it.

The Shrieking.

It has returned.

The spine-tingling scream sounds closer – closer than it did at the tree house and closer than it did at Joe's Pizza. I look to June and Dirk. They're giving me the same look in return. A look that says, 'Let's find the source of this strangeness.'

'This way!' June says.

My heart pounds in my chest as we run toward The Shrieking. I always came in dead last at the races in school – every school I ever went to, I came in last. You know how depressing that is? It means I wasn't just the slowest kid in school. I was the slowest kid in, like, *ten schools*. There is a very distinct possibility I was the slowest kid *in America*!

The Shrieking is a penetrating noise, filling my head like hornets buzzing around in my brain. And then, just like that, it stops. Where there was a chilling, slicing howl, there is now nothing. Just the sound of my heavy panting.

June leans against the rusted, bent hood of an ambulance and catches her breath. Dirk just stands.

And then another sound. One we hadn't
heard before. This one not as loud, but almost
as creepy. It's a sound almost like a burp. Like
if you burped so hard it caused your rib cage to
shatter.

'What on Earth . . .' June says.

And then it happens.

Something blocks the sun for a moment. I
think it's a flock of birds at first, but it's not.
I wish it was. Oh, how I wish it was . . .

'What is that?' Dirk says.
'Flying zombies?' June wonders.
'Down!' I shout.

Undead bodies soar through the air like they've been launched from a catapult. June drops and rolls beneath the ambulance. Dirk and I follow. We watch as limp zombie bodies pound the cement like mortar shells.

I slip the Louisville Slicer from its sheath. Zombies can take a beating. Even after falling from a serious height, they'll still get up. Their undead legs will still lift them and push them forward, so I need to be ready for their attack.

But that doesn't happen now. The zombies simply lay on the cement. Sprawled out. Dead. *Really dead.*

The zombie downpour stops as quickly as it started. I look to my friends. We all exchange very confused, very frightened looks. We slowly slip out from beneath the ambulance.

There are at least fifty of the bodies. I'm nervous to get too close. Maybe they're not *really* dead. Maybe it's some sort of strange trick. Some monstrous trap.

But they don't move – not at all.

As I inch closer, I see the full extent of the horror. There is a fist-sized hole in each zombie head. Holding my breath, covering my nose, I grab one and gently lift it closer.

Its brains have been sucked out. Its skull is now just an empty bowl.

I release the zombie. Its body drops to the ground. I almost puke right on top of it.

Dirk checks two more. 'Same,' he says. 'Brains sucked out.'

For what could be only minutes but feels like an eternity, none of us says anything. None of us even move. We just stand there, eyeing the zombies sprawled out around us.

I want to rage. I want to scream, 'WHAT IS GOING ON WHAT IS THIS SHRIEKING WHAT IS THIS HORROR?!?'

But I try to stay calm. I'm a leader.

At least, I'm trying to be.

chapter fourteen

None of us says much as we head back to the tree house. It's like there's suddenly more to this world than we ever imagined. More horror. More terror. More danger. More *everything*.

June, in a daze, flips through the radio stations. She seems to have forgotten that there is no more radio. Rough static comes from the speakers. June finally turns the knob to OFF. She rests her head against the window.

I miss music.

It's the only thing anyone says during the ride.

A big monster like Blarg? You can run from that. You can hide from that. If you have to, you can *fight* that.

But something so unknown? Something so *foul* that it sucks out the brains of the already undead? It fills us with cold, choking fear.

As Dirk pulls Big Mama into the backyard, Quint comes shuffling out of the garage, his hair a mess, shirt covered in Mountain Dew stains, like he hasn't slept in days.

But he's got a grin like the Cheshire Cat.

Before he can dive into whatever it is he's about to dive into, I stop him. We all sit down. I let June do the talking – and she details everything that happened. Everything we saw. The Shrieking, the burp, the raining zombies.

Quint slowly shakes his head. 'This is not good. However,' he continues, 'the timing is perfect. Because . . .'

I have developed a variety of zombie-catching traps. Using them, we WILL catch a zombie. And we WILL be prepared when The Shrieking shrieks again.

'And that means,' Quint says, 'it's zombie stakeout time.'

The idea of a stakeout lifts my spirits some. It helps to push the horrific vision of raining zombies to the back of my mind.

See, for as long as I can remember, I've wanted to go on a stakeout. I mean, a *real* stakeout – what's better than that? Like a cool, grizzled cop. Like buddy cops, from a buddy-cop movie! I can just picture us . . .

So we pile into Big Mama – Rover curled up in the back, weighing the whole thing down – and go hunting for snacks. You can't do a stakeout without stakeout snacks. That's like Stakeout 101.

At the grocery store, once we've filled our giant bags, June has a realization. 'Guys, since a lot of the zombies are missing – along with their brains – where do we *find* one?'

'I thought about that,' Quint says. 'And that's where Rover comes in.'

Quint kneels down in front of the big fur ball and does his best zombie impression. Rover cocks his head and looks at Quint like he's a bit bonkers. Then Rover tilts his head toward me. I shrug and do a terrible zombie impression, too.

Rover seems to understand, and moments later, he's stampeding through town. We scramble back into Big Mama, I stomp the pedal, and we follow Rover.

Rover stops at an alley that cuts between two rows of homes. Dirk steps out of Big Mama and begins examining the ground. He's in this weird, like, Apache-tracker mode. He picks up some dirt, sifts through some grass, and then holds up a finger.

'Zombie tracks,' he declares.

I frown. 'How can you tell the difference between zombie tracks and regular not-dead-person tracks?'

'It's easy . . .'

'Do the tracks appear fresh?' Quint asks.

'Since the last rain,' Dirk answers. 'Two days, maybe three.'

I have no idea how he knows this.

'Then this is the spot,' Quint declares.

I reverse Big Mama into an overrun backyard that keeps us hidden from Dozers but still lets us watch the path. Quint sets up his first trap, and with that . . .

Break out the grub! It's classic cinematic stakeout time!

Quint grins. 'I brought sunflower seeds. Ultimate stakeout food.'

Turns out, sunflower seeds must be an acquired taste.

PFFT! PFFFFT! PATEWW!

These are awful!

You ate the shells, didn't you? You're not supposed to eat the shells.

Forget the sunflower seeds. Here's the deal: being on a stakeout is all about eating really nasty, unhealthy food that clogs your arteries. That's why I've put together a sandwich I call . . . The Behemoth. Oh man, everyone's going to be so jealous.

'No energy in that garbage,' Dirk says as he eats another carrot from his garden. 'You need energy to fight monsters.'

I groan. I really didn't expect this sort of grief on a stakeout.

I'm an ants-in-the-pants kind of guy and after the first, like, forty-five minutes I decide maybe being on a stakeout isn't all it's cracked up to be.

I lift a pair of binoculars to my eyes and watch the trap. I don't spot any zombies. 'No action,' I grunt.

We're all going a little stir-crazy, so June cracks open some Fun Dip. Fun Dip's a solid post-apocalyptic food 'cause it's just coloured sugar. The stuff would probably last ten thousand years. It'll outlast roaches.

Unfortunately, we party a little too hard with the Fun Dip . . .

All the sugar is making Quint paranoid. I try telling him that, but he just bursts out, 'No, I really heard something! AGAIN! HEARD IT AGAIN!'

I cup my ear and listen, just to humour him. But I hear it, too. Shuffling. ZOMBIE shuffling!

'I think we got one . . .' I whisper.

A moment later, a zombie in a tattered Hawaiian shirt comes stumbling down the path toward Quint's trap . . .

'Yes!' Quint exclaims.

No offence to my buddy, but I kinda can't believe Quint's trap worked. Then a second later . . .

The zombie is back up, limping away on one foot and a very, very exposed shinbone. It's all sorts of awful.

Dirk giggles. Quint sighs. You'd think I would have lost my appetite, but I just inhale more Fun Dip. A one-legged zombie won't do much good for hunting down The Shrieking, so we let it go. 'Good luck out there, zombie!' I holler. 'Break a leg!'

———

'OK,' Quint says as he unloads trap #2 from the truck. 'This trap is extremely well designed and is certain to catch a zombie. It's a glue trap. *Super*glue. A zombie sets foot and *SHLUCK*. Foot equals glued.'

It's an hour before we glimpse another
zombie, this one a woman in ripped jeans and a
tattered sweatshirt. She shuffles, stops, sniffs
the air, shuffles some more, then stumbles right
into the trap . . .

'Won't have much luck following that one,
either,' June says.

Quint hangs his head. I give him an elbow to

the side. 'It's OK, buddy. At least it was scary horrific.'

'This will do the trick!' Quint says as he unloads trap #3 from the truck. Two hours and twenty-seven Fun Dip packets later . . .

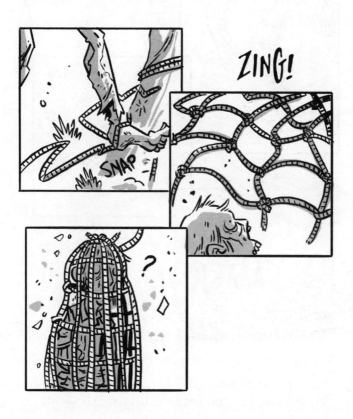

'We netted one!' I exclaim.

Quint grins and Dirk slaps him on the back. We step out of Big Mama and slowly approach. But the zombie rises, still draped in the net. Its moans turn to a confused gurgling and it begins shuffling away, faster than ever!

'This is our best chance!' I shout. 'GET HIM!'

We sprint after the brainless being. Racing around the corner, we're about to grab it, when –

RAAARRR!!!

'Winged Wretch!' June shrieks.

Winged Wretches are horrific flying villains – pure, unpolluted *evil*. The monster's razor-sharp talons grab the zombie by the shoulders. The zombie tumbles over in the net and the Winged Wretch beats its wings and thrusts upward, into the sky.

The monster's mouth opens wide – wider than I've ever seen the mouth of a Winged Wretch open. I need a pic of this – for the bestiary! I stumble back and raise my camera. No time to frame a beautiful, perfectly lit, artsy shot – I just squeeze the shutter.

Dirk grabs me by the collar, yanking me away. 'No pictures! Just running!' he shouts.

We spin and sprint (classic monster-dodging manoeuvre, the ol' spin and sprint). I feel the monster's mouth grab me – my pants rip – but I kick my feet and scoot out.

Dirk lowers his shoulder and *barrels* through
a fence, then through another, and through
another. Then we lie perfectly still until we
finally see the Winged Wretch lift off and
disappear into the distance.

'Guys,' June says, 'we stink at stakeouts.'

Quint stares at me with a wide, creepy grin and big, bright, excited eyes. I'm suddenly feeling way too naked. 'Look away, Quint. Look away.'

'No, friends!' he says excitedly. 'Our stakeout was entirely worth the effort!'

I notice he's looking at the camera resting against my hip. The image viewer shows my just-snapped pic of the Winged Wretch.

'Huh?' I say.

'I've figured it out,' Quint says. 'I now know *exactly* how to catch a zombie.'

chapter fifteen

Back at the tree house, we all tumble out of
Big Mama. Quint is *energized*, like he's been
sucking on batteries in his spare time.

He immediately retreats to his workshop with
my camera. This is the photo he's so fired up
about:

Quint says he's now certain how we can catch
(and not lose – that's important, the not losing) a
zombie. And that means we can find the source
of The Shrieking.

And that's all I care about.

Actually, also? Eating. I care about eating.
Maybe even something that's not Fun Dip.

A near-deadly run-in with a Winged Wretch will leave you seriously hungry. I find Dirk angrily yanking weeds from his vegetable garden. 'Pass me that Weed-B-Gone,' he says, pointing to a green spray bottle.

He blasts away at the weeds like they were bad-mouthing his mom or something. In seconds, the weeds shrivel away to nothing. Dirk plucks a tomato from its stem, dunks it in a bucket of rainwater, and tosses it to me.

'Y'know, I'm not a big veggie guy,' I say, taking a massive chomp. 'But this is hitting the spot.'

Dirk crunches into a carrot. 'Thought you were monster food back there.'

I thought **you** were monster food.

CHOMP

We're lucky we made it back in one piece.

Winged Wretches are no joke.

And he's right.

It's true.

Entirely, totally, terrifyingly true.

I think about that for a while. Just how lucky we are. Just how high the odds are stacked against us. All the other possible outcomes.

I catch Dirk's eye.

We're both thinking the same thing . . .

I mean, is there any way we could ever succeed here? I've blundered my way through a few monster encounters, sure – but this thing that's sucking out zombie brains? Blasting them through the air like discarded food? This thing with the power to *summon* zombies?

Just the thought of it practically has me in a state of panic-induced puking.

I make up my mind. Tomorrow we need to go back to Joe's Pizza. We need to know what the monsters think about all this.

'Friends!' Quint hollers. 'Come down here!'

I blink my eyes open. It's morning. The sun is just barely up. *Too. Early.*

This better be good, Quint, I think.

A few minutes later, I'm standing outside

Quint's workshop. He's got a big bedsheet over some giant box-looking thing. He looks like a magician about to attempt his grand finale – pull a bunch of doves from under his armpit or something.

Dirk's sitting on the ping-pong table, bouncing a ball. 'Quint, kid, just get on with it.'

Quint, totally into the magician thing, says, 'Ladies and gentlemen, I'm proud to introduce the latest and greatest in zombie catching . . .'

'That name does not exactly inspire confidence,' I say.

'I know,' he says, with a meek sigh. 'But it *is* for catching zombies. And they *are dead*. Well, technically, undead . . . but "The Cage of Undeath" doesn't have the same ring to it.'

'If you think I'm stepping in there, you're nuts,' Dirk cuts in. 'I get claustrophobic.'

Quint grins. 'No! No one need step inside! No one need risk their lives. Because of . . . REVEAL NUMBER TWO!'

With a dramatic flourish, Quint reaches inside the cage and yanks away a second sheet, revealing a sort of odd, vaguely lifelike lump.

We all inch closer. I can't lie – my curiosity is piqued. 'What on earth is that?' I ask. 'It looks like a scarecrow. Taking a nap.'

Quint laughs. 'It is, in fact, the complete opposite of a scarecrow. You might say it is an "invite crow"!'

'It looks familiar . . .' I say.

Dirk scratches his head. 'Yeah, like someone we know.'

Suddenly, June shrieks. 'ME! It looks like me! Quint, it's wearing my shirt! And pants!'

'I know!' Quint says, and he smiles like he's proud of that. 'I call it June Bait.'

- June Bait! -

'The lump smells like humans!' Quint says. 'And to the dull eyes of the zombie, this lump will look like dinner!'

'Quint, maybe you could explain *why* you stole June's clothes and dressed up a pile of junk like her?' I say. I'm trying to save Quint from getting socked in the nose here.

'It's simple!' he says. 'See . . .'

1. Zombie sniffs out the June Bait.

2. Zombie comes stumbling.

3. Zombie sees what it thinks is a human.

4. Zombie enters the cage.

5. Zombie trips this wire at bottom of cage.

6. BANG! Cage slams shut and we have a zombie!

'Easy peasy Captain Cheesy!' Quint exclaims. 'Zombie captured. I had the idea when I saw the photo of the Winged Wretch's teeth. They looked like a cage! From *Jaws*! Now let's go set it up.'

I shake my head. 'We need to go to Joe's Pizza today. After The Shrieking, after the brain-sucked zombies, I want to get Thrull's take on our sitch.'

'Fine,' Quint says. 'So we'll set the trap on the street, out front.'

Dirk drags the whole ridiculous thing across the yard and out onto Prescott Street. Quint carefully kneels down and sets the trap. With any luck, we'll have nabbed a zombie in no time.

'Bye, Fake June!' Quint calls out as we head for Joe's.

June grumbles:

I hate the June Bait.

chapter sixteen

We spot Thrull in the back, sitting with Bardle.
They're playing some sort of monster game
with big bugs – like neon-orange
cockroaches. I pull up a seat.

'Ahh, don't think I ever learned that one . . .'

'Can we retrieve you and your friends something to swallow, then?' Thrull asks.

'You mean something to eat?'

'Yes. "EAT." That is the word. Would you like? I am having őt̸t̸œr̸ĕŷę,' Thrull says as he waves something in my direction; it looks like a string of eyeballs on a wooden skewer.

Ah, you got, like, mozzarella sticks?

Thrull gives me a puzzled look.

'Y'know what,' I say. 'I actually ate before I left the house.'

Thrull shrugs and slurps down an eyeball. I see his throat bulge as it seems to become momentarily lodged in his gullet. Thrull coughs, swallows, and sucks it down. Monsters, man – not sure I'll ever get used to 'em.

'We need to talk to you guys,' I say, trying to get back to the point of the thing. 'We've seen some strange stuff recently – we figured you'd know more than we would about it.'

Thrull and Bardle exchange glances. Concerned glances, I think – though it's tough to tell with these monster faces. I'm still learning how to read all the different expressions. The only expression I definitely recognize is *hungry*.

Quint scoots his chair forward. It makes an obnoxious screeching noise. Excitedly, Quint says, 'Yesterday, my friends found a pile of zombies in the street, with their brains sucked out. Totally gone!'

Bardle leans forward. He suddenly seems not to care about the game. 'You say – with their brains removed?'

Dirk nods. 'It was gnarly.'

Bardle's strange eyes blink rapidly. One finger begins to softly tap on the table. I wonder . . . is he nervous?

'And zombies have been disappearing!' Quint says.

And then, suddenly seeming very aware that he's being watched, Bardle leans back. Is he attempting to look relaxed? 'I have no idea what this could be,' he says.

I want to state the obvious, but I'm kinda nervous. Thankfully, June isn't so shy. She says, 'It seems, well, odd that at roughly the same time you show up, this would happen. We drove past Joe's a month ago; it was empty. But now . . .' She doesn't say it accusingly or anything, but she doesn't exactly say it in the friendliest tone, either.

'That you should hear this shrieking after we arrive?' Bardle asks. 'A simple coincidence, I'm sure.'

I have to catch my breath. My heart begins slamming in my chest and I suddenly feel very anxious. What did Bardle just say? At last, I speak up. 'Um . . . Mr Bardle? None of us mentioned The Shrieking . . .'

Bardle's eyes narrow. 'No,' he says slowly. 'No, of course you didn't. I misheard.'

Behind me, I hear Dirk crack his knuckles.

Thrull's moved on from his eyeball entrée and he's now pulling the flesh off some sort of birdlike creature. He sucks it down. The smell of the charred meat is overpowering.

Bardle slowly leans back in his chair. There's a creaking sound – not sure if it's the chair or his bones. 'Just a simple misunderstanding,' he says.

The tension is so thick you could cut it open and cook it for dinner.

Thrull throws back a huge gulp of his drink and slams the empty glass down on the table. He grabs his cane – my hockey stick – and struggles to his feet. 'I have heard enough!' he barks. 'If some foul creature is dining on zombies, then I will meet this creature in battle! It puts me at risk. It puts Jack and his friends at risk. It puts *all of us* at risk. We are in this together, Bardle, are we not?'

'Of course,' Bardle says.

'Then I will find this enemy,' Thrull says matter-of-factly. 'And I will destroy it.'

Thrull takes a step, but his leg quickly gives out. He tumbles forward, tries to brace himself on a table, but the table flips and Thrull wallops into the floor.

Every monster in Joe's Pizza turns.

Bardle watches Thrull. I study his face, trying to get a read on this strange, old monster. Just as Thrull attempts to stand – and fails – I believe I see Bardle's lip twist into a slight, subtle smile.

I look away, down to Thrull. It's hard seeing this huge thing – who was once a great hunter, apparently – weakened like this.

I put out a hand and try to help Thrull to his feet, a friendly gesture that almost causes my back to give out. Five other monsters rush over and together we manage to get him back to his seat.

'Go, go, leave,' Thrull says, angrily shooing the monsters away. He quickly returns to dining on his charred bird dinner.

I feel a pain in the back of my throat – Thrull is hurt because of *us*. I wish I could go back and change what happened – that day at the mall with the Wormungulous. I wish it could have been *me* who saved my friends.

Finally, with no clue what else to do, I rap my knuckles against the table. 'We'll leave you guys to your stinky food. We have a quest to complete. By the way, Thrull – we're making great progress on the bestiary. We'll be done in no time! Thanks again for giving it to us. It's a great gift.'

I'm trying to cheer the big guy up, and it seems to work. Thrull's angry frown turns to a smile. 'Good work!' he says. 'Very good!'

'And Bardle,' I say, 'I'm sorry about the misunderstanding with the whole shrieking thing.'

Bardle waves it off. 'No matter.'

We head for the door. But as we leave, I look back at Bardle. He's staring at me. His eyes seem to penetrate my skin and seek out my soul – yeah, it's *that serious*.

I turn away.

Walking out of Joe's Pizza, my friends and I whisper.

Passing the supermarket, I pick up a rock and skim it down the road. It pings off a dented mailbox and careens off the side of an overturned Toyota. 'So now what?' I ask, feeling discouraged. 'I mean, if it's Bardle who's out there sucking zombie brains, we could be in big trouble! We could be next!'

'We don't know anything for sure,' Quint says.

'Well, we need to figure out something before we wind up –'

'UNDEAD!' Dirk exclaims.

'No, Dirk,' I say. 'Bardle won't undeadify us. He'll *real* deadify us.'

Dirk points. 'No, dude – UNDEAD! ZOMBIE! RIGHT THERE!'

And then I see. Turning the corner, we come upon our zombie trap. And –

'I can't believe it worked,' I say.

Quint grins. 'Believe it, friend! My noggin is superior!'

'I wasn't knocking your noggin.'

'Never knock my noggin.'

'WILL YOU TWO SHUT UP ABOUT NOGGINS?!' June exclaims. 'There's a zombie in a cage chewing on a stuffed fake version of ME and it is FREAKING me out.'

'Come on,' Quint says. 'quickly. Let's get it back home. With any luck, we'll soon hear The Shrieking again. And *then* we'll know who's up to what.'

'I got the snacks!' I exclaim, dashing into Quint's workshop with popcorn fresh from our fire pit. We all plop down on the couch and stare at the zombie. Sure, we've spent tons of time running from zombies, punching zombies, whacking zombies – but we've never really *studied* zombies.

'So, can I be the one to ask a stupid question?' I ask.

'You usually are,' Quint says.

'So, like . . . now that we've caught a zombie . . . can we make it our butler?'

Dirk grins. 'Zombie butler. I like it. Always wanted a butler. Nothing says class like a butler.'

'Jack, it would bite us,' Quint says. 'And then WE'D be zombies.'

'Maybe you guys,' I say. 'But I'm too quick.

'You three would get zombified and I'd have
FOUR zombie butlers. Then I'd be living the life.'

'Jack, you're insane and I love it,' June says. 'But no.'

'Fine. But I'm still calling this guy Alfred. That's my favourite butler name.'

Everyone seems just fine with Alfred.

While my friends continue to study our new zombie butler, I take Rover for a walk. I need to clear my head after the weirdness at Joe's.

I want The Shrieking to come again. But I can't make that happen. All I can do is keep busy. So when we get back home, I pull out the Louisville Slicer from its sheath, and say . . .

We've got a bestiary to complete. Let's do this.

chapter seventeen

Just because *I* want to go bestiary questing –
well, that doesn't mean my buds are with me.
They're totally focused on the brain-sucking
whatever-it-is and they seem pretty content to
ignore the bestiary and watch Alfred all day.

But after nearly a week passes with no
Shrieking, I convince Quint to pry himself free
from his Alfred studying and slap together a few
monster-hunting tools.

Once June and Dirk get a load of the killer
gadgets, they're on board with my craving for
heroic questing . . .

Tools, gang.
Tools for discovering
new monsters.

The next week is a whirlwind! A total wind of whirl! Quint keeps building new monster-hunting-and-tracking devices while Dirk, June, and I head out there – on the front lines – documenting and cataloguing these beasts.

Finding a monster, snapping a photo, watching it and documenting its behavior – you can do all that from a ways away. But getting the ESSENCE – a drop of sweat, a strand of hair – not so easy . . .

Just hold still and let me pluck one hair! C'mon! One hair! Is that so much to ask?

We search houses and stores and offices. We open mailboxes and we rummage through garages – any place in Wakefield where there might be some as-yet-undiscovered species of beastie. We even return to the Old South Graveyard, where I recover one of the Hairy Eyeball Monster's quills.

Each daily hunt unearths new creatures, both big and small. Literally . . .

Um, think I found one. . . .

Me. too!

Some of the little guys are actually kind of adorable. We find a whole furry little family of cuteness balls.

'Look at 'em!' June says, rubbing one. 'They're so fluffy.'

Dirk immediately turns into a softy. 'Let's take them home with us. They can be friends with Rover!'

But as we learn a second later, cute does *not* necessarily equal friendly.

The big monsters – the ones that are just straight-up, like, brutish behemoths – are tougher to deal with. Thankfully, Quint doesn't give us *only* tracking gadgets.

He arms us.

Arms us to the *teeth*.

I even manage to retrieve a T-shirt cannon from the high-school football supply closet. I'm kind of *obsessed* with T-shirt cannons. I went to a Boston Celtics game once, with an old foster family, and the only thing I remember was that their dancing girls blasted T-shirts up into the stands, like two hundred feet!

Quint turns our T-shirt cannon into the Glue Thrower, Goo Slower – and it's big-time helpful when we encounter the big-bellied Blobbulous down by the 7-Eleven store.

– Glue Thrower, Goo Slower –

The Blobbulous opens his blobby mouth and hurls blobby goo balls. Six double-barrel blasts of goo later, the Blobbulous is slithering away, slowed down to almost nothing, and we've got a small container loaded up with blob to show for it.

One afternoon, June declares, 'My life is missing its music.'

My stomach sinks. I'm afraid this is some very large and deep-thinking statement about her state of mind, post-apocalypse. I assume 'music' is a metaphor for happiness or joy or some sense of fulfillment.

I try to comfort her . . .

June, I'm here for you. My heart is an open comic book. Open your heart, too, and let us talk of our true feelings. The loss, the sadness, the –

Jack, I'm talking about **actual** music.

'Oh.'

'That little speaker system we have in the tree house so you can play Street Fighter in surround sound?' she asks. *'Not cutting it.* I want to dance! I need my jams!'

Well that was much less emotional than I'd hoped.

June says she had a neighbour who owned, as she describes it, 'THE BOMB SOUND SYSTEM.'

After a long day of bestiary scholaring, Dirk steers Big Mama toward June's old home. Her neighbour's front door is covered in a sticky blue-purple slime. I scoop some into one of Quint's jars. Looks like monster essence if ever I've seen it.

'You sure we want to go in here?' Dirk asks.

'You scared?' June asks, poking at him.

Dirk shrugs. 'Stinks like bad stuff in there.'

I push open the door. June wants that sound system – so we are *getting* that sound system.

What awaits us inside is revolting. Quint built us about eighty-seven gadgets, but not a single one for battling overpoweringly pungent and unpleasant odours.

The walls are crawling with insects. But these aren't potato bugs or roaches or cicadas or any of that Earth stuff. This is *beyond* that. Ever see one of those Discovery Channel shows about the world's weirdest creatures? You know, microscopic bugs with twenty dozen arms?

Imagine that, but, like, triple the weirdness level.

The walls seem to move and crawl. The floor is like one long, trembling carpet. Maggoty creatures roll around. Clicking, clacking tentacle bugs scurry about.

'Nope,' Dirk says, speaking through his T-shirt, which he has pulled up over his nose. 'No surround sound system is worth this.'

'But it's right there!' June says. She points to the living room, just down the hall.

Despite the awfulness, we *do* have a chance here to collect samples of a whole plethora of putrid pests. 'You guys grab the stereo,' I say. 'I'm going to study some insects. And try not to puke in the process.'

As they creep down the hall, I begin using Quint's Essence Collector Gadget.

I hate this, I hate this, I hate this!

I spot a trail of slime that disappears beneath a double swinging door. The kitchen, I assume.

Holding my breath, I push open the door. The walls *slither*. Every inch of floor, every inch of cabinet, every inch of counter is teeming with monstrous maggots.

As soon as I step inside, the insects begin to gather themselves. Amassing, assembling, joining together to form something nightmarish.

Vomit begins to rush up my throat. I try to run, but the horror in front of me is too much . . .

Suddenly, I'm lifted off my feet. It's Dirk! 'We gotta get outta here, kid!' he barks.

'Uh-huh, uh-huh,' I manage.

June cradles two huge speakers and Dirk cradles me as we race out the front door. A sound follows us: a splattery sort of wet explosion.

We dash back to Big Mama and then race straight home. I don't say anything, and neither do they – but we all know: this time, THEY saved ME.

I would have been eaten without them. I'd be freakin' insect chow!

Maybe my friends don't need me as much as I thought. Maybe it's really *me* who needs *them*.

Maybe I *can* just trust them to stay alive on their own. But still . . . what if I do, and then they get hurt? Or eaten? Or chopped up? Or zombified?

Then what?

Back at the tree house, Dirk and June set up the speakers. There will be a dance party, June announces.

'They can dance all they want,' I think. As long as they keep themselves safe. And as long as they're there to save *my butt* when my butt is in need of saving.

And me? I'm going to shower for about seventeen hours. And I'm never reading another Ant-Man comic again.

Our quest is exhausting. Part dangerous, part terrifying, part fascinating, frantic fun.

But I can't stop. Because once I stop – then I begin to think about The Shrieking. The Shrieking and the image that I can't shake: the image of zombies with their brains sucked out.

All I can do is wait. Wait with Alfred. Wait for The Shrieking to return so we can solve this mystery . . .

We're all lying out in the backyard on a cloudy afternoon, reviewing the bestiary, adding an entry for a weirdo monster I've named the Toe Tower, when we turn the page and realize . . .

It's complete.

'We're done,' Dirk says.

June grins proudly. 'Two hundred and thirty-two entries.'

Almost three weeks after the hunt began, we're bruised and battered and exhausted – but the bestiary is finished.

QUEST COMPLETE!

Our search for the source of The Shrieking, though?

No progress has been made. We've not heard a peep.

But I'm waiting.

I grip my blade when I sleep, because I know, soon enough, the villain will present itself . . .

And I will be ready.

chapter eighteen

It's past midnight. The moon is big in the sky –
a blood moon, I think they call it – and rays of
blue light shine through the windows.

Dirk and June are fast asleep, but I can't

snooze, so Quint and I are playing Mario Kart. I'm coming out of a power slide when I hear something. At least, I think I hear it. I click START.

'Hey, you paused it!' Quint exclaims. 'Just as I was going over the big jump! Not fair, friend! I'm going to come out of the jump into the turn and –'

'Shh!' I say. 'Dude, you hear that?'

'The only thing I heard was you robbing me of a red shell,' Quint says.

I turn off the TV. I could have sworn I heard something. But all I hear now is the rumbling of the generator. I step out to the deck and switch it off. The generator chokes and coughs and burps smoke – and then goes quiet.

Quint peeks out the door. 'What is it?'

'Maybe my mind was playing tricks on me . . .' I start, but I'm interrupted by a banging and clanging sound, followed by a loud, choked moaning.

Quint and I look at each other, confused, and then both at the same time realize –

'Alfred!'

We hurry down to the garage . . .

Our brainless butler tries to walk forward but simply bangs his head against the cage.

'It's like he's in a trance,' Quint says. 'I wonder if he hears The Shrieking?'

'Well, I don't hear it. Do *you* hear it?'

'No –'

But then it comes. The angry, ferocious scream fills the air once again.

It's time to release Alfred and get to the bottom of this mystery. But what if we let him go and we lose him? I know he's just a zombie, but he's *our* zombie.

I look to Quint – he's smiling like he's reading my mind. He holds up a bike helmet. On the back is a bright flashing light. 'No way we'll lose him in the crowd with this,' Quint says.

I nod. 'Good thinking.'

'You get the helmet on Alfred,' Quint says as he rushes out of the room. 'We need to hurry before The Shrieking ends. I'll wake Dirk and June.'

'No, no,' I quickly say. 'Don't get June and Dirk. I don't – I don't want to risk them.'

Quint eyes me.

Looking to the floor, trying to dodge his guilt-tripping gaze, I remember how June and Dirk saved me from the insect monster. How I'd be done-zo without them. And I remember, trying to go it alone – that's a good way to end up, well, *not alive anymore* . . .

'Right, good idea, Quint,' I finally say. 'Grab 'em.'

Quint gives me a big thumbs-up, then turns – leaving me alone with Alfred. OK . . . Um. Sure. No problem. Just need to put a helmet on a zombie.

I step close to his cage. 'Hey, Alfred! You're going to help us save the day. I just need to let you out without you eating me, OK . . .?' I trail off as I try to figure out how to go about this.

When Quint returns with Dirk and June, the three of them all burst out laughing. I'm perched on top of the cage, gripping the helmet, trying to figure out how to simultaneously open the door and drop the helmet on Alfred's head.

'June, I could use your help here,' I say. 'Distract him.'

'How do you expect me to distract him?'

'Fine, fine,' I say. 'Everyone – behind the cage. I'll open it and drop the helmet.'

That works. The door swings open with a clang. Quickly I yank my hand away and drop the helmet on Alfred's rotten noggin. The light on the back of the helmet flashes as Alfred shuffles toward the front gate.

I jump off the cage, race up to the tree house, slip on a pair of Quint-designed chain-metal action gloves (for avoiding zombie bites), grab the Louisville Slicer, and a moment later . . .

We take Big Mama. Dirk drives slowly through Wakefield, staying a block or two behind Alfred the whole way. This time we're being smart. And we are NOT entering any graveyards.

I check the dashboard clock. It's nearly one in the morning. We've been driving for almost an hour. And still, The Shrieking continues. And still, Alfred shuffles.

Soon the street is thick with the undead. There are more here than I've seen in a month. Ever since the zombies started vanishing.

June gasps. 'It *is* like a parade.'

'And not the fun kind with balloons,' I mutter. 'This is no New Year's Day Parade.'

Near the edge of the town, a narrow, two-lane bridge crosses over a trickling river. Past the river is a forest. We're not too far from the spot where, weeks back, we got caught in that sudden brain-sucked-zombie downpour.

We wait for all the zombies to cross the bridge, then Dirk slowly steers across.

Thick trees loom over us, with beams of moonlight shining through. It's not the most inviting sight. 'We'll have to hoof it from here,'

I say, barely hiding the unease in my voice. We leave Big Mama at the edge of the forest and step inside.

There must be two hundred zombies moving through the woods, en masse. The way they move with this single-mindedness, you'd think someone was handing out free flesh dinners.

I keep my eye on the flashing light of Alfred's helmet as we trek through the woods. We've been walking for nearly an hour when June taps me on the shoulder, points, and says, 'Up ahead. A clearing.'

We sneak forward.

The Shrieking is at its loudest now. It rattles off the trees and practically penetrates my soul.

And then I see it.

The source.

The thing we've been hunting.

I go woozy. It's like I have Sprite bubbles in my head. Dirk grabs my arm.

It is a tree. It sits at the entrance of the clearing. The Shrieking is coming *from the tree*.

But this tree is not like any tree anyone has ever seen before – not on this Earth . . .

It rises out of the ground like a gnarled hand, white and twisted and covered in throbbing,

pulsating Vine-Thingies. The branches
are like bones. The wood is rotted. The
tree itself almost seems zombified. Like
it rotted away but never actually *died*.

At the bottom, a gaping chasm has formed
in the trunk, almost like a mouth. The
Shrieking seems to come from there: from
the wind, passing through the strange,
jagged arch of twisted timber.

'The Vine-Thingies,' Dirk says, staring up at the twisting tentacles protruding from the branches. 'The Vine-Thingies are part of it.'

And then, with blood-chilling horror, we see *why* the zombies have been beckoned. As each zombie stumbles into the clearing, the tree's branches move and shift. The branches snap and reach down in a series of chilling, herky-jerky movements. Next the Vine-Thingies lash out, grab the zombies, and pull them into the air. The branches open at the end, like ferocious wooden mouths – and they inhale the zombies.

'It's . . . it's eating the zombies . . .' June says.

And with each swallowed zombie, the bark cracks and snaps and the tree swells and bulges. The zombies are food. The tree is growing.

A cracking, wooden burp sound erupts. The ground shakes and the top of the tree rips open and . . .

'That's why zombies were raining down on us before!' June says. 'When this tree finishes sucking up their brains, it spits them out.'

'Picky eater for a monster tree,' I say.

And then another sound. This one louder than the devouring of zombies. It's an unearthly, inhuman kind of chanting sound.

The clouds shift. The moon shines brighter. And that's when we see it. There is a creature on its knees, in front of the tree. Strange, foreign, monstrous words erupt from the creature's lungs.

We all realize, together, with a sudden gasp – the chanting creature is Thrull.

chapter nineteen

Thrull?

What would Thrull be doing here? *Bardle* was the one who seemed to have some hidden knowledge of The Shrieking.

'Oh no!' June says, snapping me back to attention. 'Alfred!'

Through the trees, I spot Alfred's flashing bicycle helmet. He's shuffling into the clearing. Shuffling in, to be eaten . . .

My butler! No evil tree eats my butler!

Quint grabs at my shirt. 'Jack, no.'

I shake him off and begin sneaking around the edge of the clearing. Every other moment there's a sickening *SCHLURP* and a howling moan as another zombie brain is devoured by the tree. Thrull's chanting grows louder and louder . . .

I tiptoe out into the clearing. I come up behind Alfred like I'm doing some Assassin's Creed-type stuff, but I'm not executing him –

I'm saving him. I flex my fingers, feel the chain mail against them, and then –

Alfred instantly bites down on my hand – and I really, really hope Quint's chain-mail gloves are as strong as he promised. Alfred's heels trace two rough tracks in the dirt as I drag him back into the darkness.

When every last zombie has been swallowed – except for Alfred – Thrull stops chanting and begins to speak. And what he says is just – wow . . .

I gasp.

Holy. Ravioli.

Ṛeżżőch the Ancient? That's the bad dude
Bardle was talking about. And Thrull is trying
to bring him *here?!?*

Thrull is a servant of Ṛeżżőch the Ancient,
just like Blarg was! And Thrull is using *this tree*
to bring Ṛeżżőch into our world!

The trunk seems to pull apart, cracking and widening the chasm.

The splinters around the edges glow red and blue as beams of energy begin to jump back and forth between them.

In this strange window of glimmering, flickering light, a dim, blurry face appears. An inhuman face. And as it begins to speak, I realize, with horror – I'm staring at the face of Ŗeżżőcħ the Ancient, calling to Thrull from another dimension.

I look across the way to Quint and mouth, 'Key?'

Quint just shrugs.

'Ŗeżżőcħ, my lord,' Thrull says. 'I am your servant.'

'WHAT OF THE KEY?' the voice repeats. **'I MUST REACH THIS WORLD, AND I CANNOT UNTIL YOU OPEN THE DOOR.'**

'A group of human children are completing a bestiary,' Thrull says. 'I have filled the bestiary with magical energy. When the bestiary is full, the essence of the creatures inside will transform the book into the key.'

There's a hard lump in my throat as realization floods through me . . .

Thrull used us!

'I HUNGER,' Ŗeżżőcħ says. **'OUR OLD WORLD IS BARE. WHEN I ENTER THIS NEW WORLD, I MUST EAT.'**

'Yes, Ŗeżżőcħ,' Thrull says. 'There are many monsters close by that you can feast upon. I have gathered them. They know nothing of this. I alone am your servant.'

Does he mean the monsters at Joe's? Are they in cahoots with Thrull – or is he going to feed his friends to Ŗeżżőcħ?!

'**GOOD,**' the voice growls. '**GOOOOOD. SOOOOON. SOOOOON YOU SHALL BRING ME FORTH . . .**'

And with that, the energy snaps away. The tree crackles and the window closes and the branches become still. This strange, evil, magical ceremony is over.

Thrull uses my hockey stick to slowly stand.

Seeing that, it hits me.

That's why Thrull was at the mall! He was hunting for monsters to fill the bestiary himself. And *that's* why the bestiary already had entries in it when Thrull gave it to us.

But then he was injured. Thrull's injury is no trick. He knew he could not fill the bestiary by himself anymore. And then the moment he saw the Louisville Slicer, the moment he realized that I 'felled' Blarg – he *knew* we could help.

Upon receiving the bestiary, we began doing his foul deeds for him. We were never simply documenting or recording. We were loading the magic book up with monster essence – so the book could become this key! A key to open this door-tree-thing!

I've been a pawn in Thrull's game. I've never felt so foolish, so naive – and so furious.

Footsteps bring me back to the present. Thrull is walking to the edge of the clearing.

I step further into the shadows.

He limps past me.

And I smell it.

I don't smell any cheap aftershave cover-up. I smell *Thrull*.

And his scent his pure evil. The same scent as Blarg.

I hold my breath as he turns to look back. His strange, inhuman eyes stare into the darkness. I can almost feel his gaze upon me.

Finally, he turns and tramps his way through the woods.

chapter twenty

I jam a sweaty sock in Alfred's mouth so no one gets bitten, and we run, run, run. We don't stop running until we get back to Big Mama. It's nearly dawn when Dirk gets us home to the tree house. We stumble out of the truck and collapse in the grass: pained, tired, terrified.

I'm relieved to be home. But I'm NOT relieved knowing that our time on Earth – the time *of* Earth – is going to be very, very, very short if we don't act quickly. And by act, I of course mean act like awesome, fist-flinging, sword-swinging heroes.

I climb up into the tree house. Inside, I slip the key into the snack lockbox. The rattling sound echoes in the morning quiet. I open it and stare down at the bestiary.

What have I done?

Frantic, I flip open the bestiary and begin tearing at the pages, trying to pry the essence loose, trying to rip it to shreds. But it doesn't work – instead, I feel something like electricity shoot through me and I leap back.

Quint comes rushing in behind me, reminding me there's no time for feeling sorry, no time for regrets, no time for *anything* but action – and maybe, hopefully, a chocolate chip mini-muffin or two.

'Lord of the Rings, Jack? That isn't real,' June says as she comes through the door. 'That's a fantasy novel!'

'Um. Did you not just see the giant talking tree and the monster servant?!' I exclaim. 'It couldn't have been any more Lord of the Rings-y if there were CGI orcs running around and white-bearded Magneto wizards!'

June nods. 'Yup. Yup. Fair point.'

Dirk comes in behind June. He rips the bestiary from my hand. 'I will punch the book into nothing!' he roars.

After, like, the nineteenth punch, Dirk
collapses. His knuckles are bright red. 'That
didn't work.'

I leap up onto the poker table. I grip the
Louisville Slicer and bring it crashing down.
It slams into the book – but I take the brunt of
the blow. The tip of the blade splinters and I'm
thrown backward, off the table.

June looks to Quint. 'I think we need more
firepower.'

'On it,' Quint replies.

Nothing.

No change.

I turn to my friends. My shoulders are slack. All of us have realized the same thing: this is TOTALLY a Lord of the Rings thing and the bestiary is TOTALLY INDESTRUCTIBLE and we're TOTALLY DOOMED.

'Maybe we could just hide it,' Dirk says. 'Bury it somewhere where Thrull will never find it.'

I shake my head. 'Thrull will come for us. If we don't have the bestiary, he'll feed us to that crazy Tree of Entry! Or something worse than a tree! Like, monster bushes or hedges or shrubs!'

I can think of only one other option. One crazy, last-ditch attempt. 'Guys,' I say, 'if we can't destroy the book . . . then we have to destroy the tree.'

chapter twenty-one

I turn around, silently cursing myself. *Just great, Jack. Just great. Offer up all sorts of answers, but no solutions. Some hero . . .*

I step out onto the deck, lean over the railing, and sigh deeply. And that's when I see it: Dirk's garden.

An idea is forming. I spin around. 'Dirk, what's been driving you the most nuts these past weeks?'

'Besides you guys?'

'Very funny. For real.'

Dirk shrugs. 'I guess the weeds messing with my garden.'

'And how have you been dealing with these weeds?' I ask.

'Been using a spray bottle of weed killer I found at that zombie dude's house down the block.'

That's what we need. Weed killer! Like, an industrial-sized, metric mass load! And then we – BOOM! – blow up the tree with it!

Where are we going to get a 'metric mass load' of weed killer?

No one's going to like this. I brace myself for a head-butt.

'We have to go back to the mall,' I say. 'To Lowe's, where Dirk got his gardening supplies. I doubt in the mad looting rampage panic after the Monster Apocalypse anyone was like, "Honey, don't forget to stock up on weed killer!"'

'I'm pretty sure the Wormungulous LIVES at the mall,' June points out. 'Going back there is probably not smart.'

I look around. No one looks particularly eager to square off with that giant worm again. Not that I blame them.

Quint says, 'I had actually drawn up a number of plans and scenarios for how we might re-enter the mall . . .'

I light up. Hope! 'Great, Quint! And . . .?'

'Each one ends in the same horrible, painful death . . .'

I plop down on the ground. I'm staring at the June Bait and Alfred and the cage.

And it hits me.

I have a solution.

But I don't feel relieved.

Now I'm even more terrified. I'm terrified because I know exactly what I have to do next. I know exactly how we can get into the mall and get a metric mass load of weed killer.

It requires me, inside Alfred's cage.

Acting as bait for the Wormungulous.

chapter
twenty-two

It's just past noon, and we're all in Big Mama,
headed for the Circle One Mall. Alfred's empty
cage rattles in the back of the truck. Our butler is
back home, locked inside the garage. He's served
his purpose, so we could just let him free – but I'm
worried that he'll get his brains sucked out by the
tree. What kind of butler-having guy would I be if
I let my butler's brains get sucked? The bad kind of
butler-having guy, that's what.

OK, explain
the plan.

It's simple.
Super simple.

'I'm going to get inside Alfred's cage. You guys will leave me in it, inside the mall – at the food court. You hide a safe distance away, in the parking lot. The Wormungulous will smell me or sense me or whatever it does – and it'll come for me. The fact that I haven't showered in a week should help. You with me so far?'

'Yes, we're with you,' June says. 'And yes, you do need to shower.'

'As soon as he comes, I'll radio you guys on this,' I say, holding up one of our walkies. 'While the Wormungulous is busy with me, you get your butts to Lowe's and load up Big Mama with weed killer.'

'What if the Wormungulous simply swallows the cage whole?' Quint asks.

'I just have to take that risk,' I say.

'Take that risk?!' Quint exclaims. 'That's a very large risk, friend.'

I shoot him a hard look. 'Do any of you have a better plan?'

And with that, everyone shuts up.

This isn't about us.

It's about everyone else who's still alive: the humans we haven't met but *have* to assume are out there, the monsters at Joe's whom Thrull would feed to Ŗeżžőch, the world itself.

'All right, then,' Dirk says. 'It's a plan.'

June squeezes my shoulder. 'We'll see you soon.'

And with that, my friends are gone. They pile into Big Mama and drive across the parking lot.

But the Wormungulous does not show up.

June soon buzzes in over the walkie.

'Everything OK in there?'

'Yep. Just waiting. Know any good jokes to keep me busy?'

'When do zombies go to sleep?'

I groan. This'll be awful. 'When?'

'When they're dead tired!'

'Terrible. You can never give me grief about my bad jokes again,' I say.

I'm picking a hangnail when June buzzes back and hums the *Countdown* theme. I laugh. I like my friends. I hope I live to see them again . . .

After forty-five minutes, I decide it's time to make a move. The world is at stake here – we can't just be hanging out in cages, picking at hangnails, humming classic game show theme songs.

So I open the cage door.

Breath held, teeth clenched, I step out into the deserted food court. I pull the Louisville Slicer from my sheath, raise it high, and slam it into the floor. I do it again, over and over.

BAM!

BAM!

BAM!

BAM!

On the fifth bam, I hear something crashing, far away – at the other end of the mall.

I slam the blade into the floor again.

BAM! BAM! BAM!

Another crash.

Glass shattering. I see it . . .

Ahead of me, the floor is bending and breaking as the Wormungulous hurtles toward me. The ground at my feet bends and twists and shatters.

KA-KA-KRAKKK!!!!

There's a seismic-type shift, the floor splits, and it appears . . .

WORM BURST!!!

Metal gates covering nearby storefronts shatter as the monster moves toward me, emitting an ear-piercing shriek.

'GO, GUYS, GO!' I shout into the walkie. 'NOW!'

'DRIVING!' June responds.

I wheel around and race back to the cage, but the worm blasts past and cuts in front of me. The floor crumbles and bends. My stomach flips as I'm lifted up into the air!

Words scream inside my head: 'GET IN THE CAGE, JACK! GET IN THE CAGE, JACK! GET IN THE CAGE, JACK! GET IN THE CAGE, JACK!'

The Wormungulous's back is slimy and slick and covered in small tentacles. Gripping one, I manage to gain my footing.

I scramble forward, then leap! My body slams into the cage and the door clangs shut behind me.

KA-SLAM!

The cage lands upside down and my head bangs into the metal bottom. There's blood on my lips – it tastes like pennies.

My eyes blink open.

The Wormungulous circles, thundering through the food court. It screams past the cage and turns, looping around. It's wrapping around the cage like an oversized, ultra-awful anaconda.

And that's when I realize: I'm going to be crushed.

chapter
twenty-three

I feel like I'm in the trash compactor in *Star Wars*.

But then, suddenly, the Wormungulous moans. A pained wail escapes from its lungs and the monster goes slack. The cage bars release. It's like the monster is suddenly out of breath.

I see why.

There's a long scar running along the side of its body. The cage scrapes and rubs against it.

No.

I'm mistaken.

It's not a scar – it's an open, festering wound from where I sliced it weeks earlier, when I battled it.

The Wormungulous's face is dotted with eyes and all of them are wet and all of them are watching me.

Guilt tugs at my insides. I bite my lip. The Wormungulous does not emit the stench of evil. It smells nothing like Blarg. It smells nothing like Thrull. It smells nothing like Dozers or Winged Wretches.

At last, I lift open the handle and push the cage open. The door presses against the monster's side. It moans softly.

I look at the long wound across his side.

I did that.

Me, I think, with a thickness in my throat.

I imagine the moment, months earlier, when doors were flung open and monsters were propelled into our dimension. And this monster was just plucked from its home and happened to land here.

I know what it feels like to be yanked from your home – it's confusing and scary.

No wonder it tried to eat us.

I hear the screech of tyres. Big Mama hurtles inside the mall and comes to a stop. 'JACK!' June screams, rushing out of the truck. 'WHAT ARE YOU DOING?'

Guys, come here. I want to help it.

Minutes later, we're gathered around the monster. Everyone is on edge. At any moment, it could turn furious and devour us.

'June?' I ask. 'Any chance you know how to sew?'

'What, 'cause I'm a girl, you just assume I know how to sew?'

I shrug. 'Moms know how to do that stuff.'

'I'm not a mom!'

'I can do it,' Dirk says.

We all eye the big guy.

'So what?' Dirk says. 'Yeah, I know how to sew, OK? I've sewn up my clothes for years.'

'Hey, all good, buddy,' I say. 'You sew and you garden. Right on.'

Dirk continues, 'But we need a big needle. And a lot of thread. This is one mighty cut.'

Where do we find a needle to sew up a giant monster with? After a moment, Dirk's eyes light up and he says, 'The Louisville Slicer.'

I pull it from its sheath. 'Really?'

'Yeah, I just need to rip off a shard to use as a needle.'

'Rip off a shard?!' I exclaim. 'You want to tear off a hunk of my most iconic tool of monster destruction?!'

'You want to fix this guy up or not?' Dirk asks.

I swallow and hand over the blade. 'Yes I do. I want to fix the guy up . . .'

June tosses Dirk some coiled-up rope from the bed of Big Mama, and he goes to work . . .

Hang on, big guy. You'll feel better soon.

'How did you know?' June finally asks me.

'Huh?'

'You left the cage. How did you know it would be safe? We thought your brain broke or something.'

I shrug. 'It just . . . it seemed hurt, like it needed help.'

The Wormungulous trembles and shudders as Dirk inserts the makeshift needle into its skin, then runs it through the wound and out the other side. Dirk continues like this, sewing up the entire ten-foot-long gash. The worm whimpers.

'This is good, worm guy,' I say, running my hand over him. 'It doesn't feel like it, but it is.'

When Dirk finishes the final stitch, he's covered in wet yellow worm gunk. He's scrubbing off his hands in the coin fountain when the Wormungulous lets out a long, deep bellow. The floor crumbles and the monster dives through it. It's graceful, almost – like a shark slipping beneath the water.

chapter
twenty-four

Back home, we get Alfred into his cage. Then, I
examine the weed killer. We have nine GIANT
JUGS of something called Walt's Weed-B-Gone.

'I'm going to hook hoses up to the weed
killer,' Quint says. 'We'll run the hoses to Super
Soakers. And then we blast away at the tree.'

I begin climbing up into the tree house to
retrieve the space marine suit. I have a feeling
we might need it. But halfway up the ladder, I
stop. Looking at the garage, I watch Quint lose
control of the hose and spray water everywhere.
June's hair is soaked. She laughs. Dirk grabs
Quint and lifts him up into the air, pretending
he's about to unleash one of John Cena's Five
Moves of Doom. Quint and Dirk both giggle.

I can't lose these guys.

I'd rather lose *myself* than lose them.

I finish climbing up into the tree house – and I
immediately gag. I throw my hand over my nose

and mouth. A thick, acidic scent fills the air, like burnt brownies and sidewalk chalk.

The smell of evil. The smell of Thrull.

The tree house interior is pitch-black somehow, even though it's the middle of the day. It's like all light has been sucked from the room.

Slowly, a dim light returns. And I see him . . .

I gulp. Need to play this freeze-pop cool. 'Hey, Thrull! Long time no see. You just, ah, let yourself right in, huh? I didn't even realize you knew where we lived.'

'I know many things,' Thrull says.

'Right.'

Suddenly, Thrull grins. 'I haven't seen you guys around Joe's Pizza in a few weeks, so I thought I'd pop in and pay you a visit. How's the bestiary coming?'

I swallow hard. I can feel the fear on my face – I need to hide it. I try cracking a smile, but I'm sure I just look like the Joker.

We kinda lost interest in the bestiary. We've been doing other stuff.

Lots of Frisbee, actually. Ultimate Frisbee. You play? Thinking about putting together a post-apocalyptic Ultimate Frisbee team. I was maybe gonna put up a flyer at Joe's.

Any interest?

COOL SHRUG

Thrull lowers his head and chuckles softly. When he raises it again, his eyes are narrowed and seem to glow red. He speaks in a thick, wet growl. 'Jack, where is the key?'

I gulp. We were so careful! We hid. We covered our tracks. Maybe if I play dumb . . .

'Ah, the key?' I ask.

'The bestiary,' Thrull growls.

'Um, Thrull,' I say, 'I'm really *not sure* what you're talking about. Is everything OK?'

Thrull's beady eyes look me up and down. If he gets his hands on the bestiary, he only needs to bring it to the tree. And then he will perform the ceremony and the bestiary will open the Tree of Entry – and we're done for. Reżżőch will come. Everything, kaput.

'Do not lie,' he says. 'I know you were at the Tree of Entry. Reżżőch the Ancient saw you. He sees all.'

'The book is gone,' I say after a long moment. 'We destroyed it.'

Thrull laughs. It's a harsh sound, like footsteps on gravel. 'No human can destroy an enchanted bestiary. Your lies are foolish. You speak nonsense. Tell me where it is. Now.'

'OK, you're right,' I say. 'I lied. But for real –

for truth – we lost it. Actually, to be specific, I lost it.'

Thrull says nothing.

'I'm like, y'know, super absentminded. You should have seen my locker back in school. You know – before your evil overlord opened the portal door thing and the monsters came and DESTROYED the joint. But yeah, my locker was just papers and old sandwiches everywhere. So I just, y'know, lost the bestiary. Misplaced it. I swear sometimes, if my head wasn't attached to my shoulders . . .'

Thrull rises. He fills the room.

I want to step back. I want to cower in the corner. I want to cry.

But I don't do any of that.

Instead, slowly, I reach back and grip the handle of the Louisville Slicer.

A cruel smirk appears on Thrull's lips. 'Is this where you want your life to end, Jack?'

Before I can respond, June calls from the garage, 'JACK! LET'S GO! YOUR HELP IS NEEDED!'

Thrull grins. 'Call your friends up here.'

'No.'

'Call them.'

I clench my teeth so hard I half expect them to shatter inside my mouth. 'I. Will. Not.'

Thrull stomps toward me. I back up, trip, and tumble into the corner. 'Call them,' he growls again, as his thick paws grab hold of me.

'F-f-fine,' I manage to choke out. My shoulders sag. My head lowers. And then –

QUINT! RUN! GET EVERYONE! GO! THRULL IS HERE!

Thrull scowls. 'You will pay for that. Pay dearly.' With a sudden whip and crash, I'm thrown *through* the tree house wall. Wood splinters and shatters. A second later I crash-land in a pile of leaves. That's probably what keeps me from, y'know, breaking every bone in my body.

My knee slams into my nose and pain shoots up through my brain. First thing I think: I am *super* delighted we never raked the backyard.

I spit out a leaf and get to my feet.

I see Thrull leaping down from the tree house. Pain on his face as he braces himself with my hockey stick.

But at least I was able to alert my friends. With any luck, they're blocks away now, running.

Or not . . .

Turn around, Thrull. And go.

'Aww, c'mon guys,' I shout. 'I told you to run!'

Dirk shakes his head. 'Not leaving you, dork.'

June holds her broom spear to Thrull's chest. 'We stick together.'

'You are foolish. All of you,' he growls. 'You don't understand the power I wield. I'm a servant of Ṛeżżŏċh the Ancient, Destructor of Worlds.'

Dirk raises his fist and charges. Thrull backhands him – a slap that sends Dirk sprawling into Rover so that they both land in a heap.

June jabs at him, but her spear only shatters against Thrull's chest.

Quint shrieks, 'Leave us alone!' With no weapon, no nothing – just a bit of plucky resolve, as they say – he jumps at Thrull. The monster snatches him out of the air and holds him up high.

TELL ME WHERE THE BESTIARY IS, JACK, OR YOUR FRIEND DIES. HERE. NOW. YOU HAVE ONE SECOND.

'The lockbox! In the tree house!' The words burst from my mouth without hesitation.

'Jack, no!' Quint squeaks.

Thrull looks to June. 'Get the box. Now.'

June hangs her head and crosses to the tree house ladder. A moment later she's climbing back down, lockbox tucked beneath her arm. I shudder as she gives it to Thrull.

With his free hand, Thrull squeezes the box. Metal crunches and it pops open. The bestiary falls to the grass. A smile creeps across Thrull's face as he picks it up.

He examines the pages and sees that it's complete. 'Wonderful work,' he says with a taunting leer. 'I had hoped you would make progress while my leg healed. But I never thought you'd complete the book. Impressive. You are to be commended.'

Man oh man, do I ever want to knock this dude out.

Thrull's eyes go to the garage and the zombie cage. 'In,' he barks.

I look to June nervously.

Thrull squeezes Quint's neck.

'In,' Thrull says again.

I slowly walk to the cage. When I open it,

Alfred shuffles out. He immediately lunges for me. Some butler . . .

Thrull snatches up Alfred and flings him across the yard like he's one of Rover's chew toys. Alfred crashes through the fence. I watch as he rises and stumbles away. I hope he's safe out there. I know he's brain-dead, but I'll miss the guy . . .

'I want you wide awake when your world ends,' Thrull says to me. 'Not a zombie. Go. Forward.'

I step inside. Thrull nods to Dirk and June. They follow, slipping in until we're all packed together like sardines. Then Thrull closes and locks the door.

'Now put Quint down!' I say.

Thrull shakes his head. 'I think not. Too smart, this one. Might figure out an escape. But you three – I doubt that very much.'

I shriek and curse and scream and rattle the bars, but it does nothing except make Thrull's grin grow wider and more horrific.

Tapping the bestiary with one fat finger, Thrull says, 'Goodbye, children. And thank you for your help in bringing forth Ŗeżżőcħ the Ancient. Your participation in the end of your world is greatly appreciated.'

With that, Thrull rips the roof of Big Mama clean off and tosses Quint into the back. Thrull slides into the seat. He jams his finger into the ignition, and somehow, the engine roars to life. A moment later, he's off . . .

chapter twenty-five

I sink to the floor. My chin falls to my chest, my arms go limp, and my head spins like a manic merry-go-round.

I've failed.

I look at my friends. Sweat pours from Dirk's pale face.

I failed.

I failed.

June says something, but I don't hear her. Every sound seems to be a mile away. It's like I'm listening to the world from underwater.

I pride myself on being a cool, calm, never-panicked hero – but right now I'm way far from that.

'Is it stuffy in here?' I ask. I feel my mouth moving, but I don't hear myself speaking.

I see June's face. She's shaking me, trying to help. I look to Dirk. He has his eyes shut tight and his hands wrapped around his knees. He's rocking back and forth.

Stale air in the garage. I smell oil and sawdust. I smell melted plastic. I smell gasoline.

Need water.

Need something cold.

June snaps her fingers in my face.

I can barely see her. It's like looking at something through 120-degree heat – wavy and out of focus.

Then a whistle. High-pitched, cutting through the air. June whistling.

Why?

I shut my eyes again. Sink back against the bars.

And then something cool and wet on my face. Water?

It brings me to. Wakes me up. Snaps me out of it. I gasp for air, sucking in a huge breath.

I see Rover. His big tongue out, licking me. Cooling me. Sounds come back. It no longer feels like I'm drowning in dread.

June is in my face, looking me over. 'Jack? Jack, you all right?'

'Yes,' I say slowly. 'Yes, I'm OK. Sorry – just – a little freaked there for a second. Felt like the world was closing in around me.'

'You good?' June asks.

'I'm good.'

'You ready to figure a way out of here?'

'I'm ready.'

Dirk grabs the bars and shakes. They won't break. They won't bend. Instead . . .

My camera clanks off my head. It turns on as it hits me, bringing up the pic of us with Thrull and Bardle. It was just a month ago, but it feels like ages. I thought we had monster allies. But no – just more monster enemies.

Well, one monster enemy: Thrull.

'Are the other monsters bad?' June asks, like she's thinking what I'm thinking.

'I don't think so. I was suspicious of Bardle. But it seems Thrull's the real villain, if he's planning to feed the rest of them to Ŗeżżőcħ the Ancient once it comes to Earth.'

'Then we'll just have to trust the rest of them. Because we need help.' June holds up the camera and taps the image of Bardle. 'Rover, can you find this guy?'

Rover's big monster eyes narrow. His head lifts. He looks at me. I nod. 'Please, Rover. Please.'

Rover turns and darts through the garage door. June looks at me. 'Fingers crossed.'

'Fingers and toes,' I reply.

———

An hour passes. No Rover. No Bardle.

'How will the world end, do you think?' June asks. 'This Ŗeżżőcħ guy. What will he do?'

I shrug. 'Maybe he'll be like a Tasmanian devil thing, raging across the planet . . .'

'Maybe he'll sit on a big throne,' June says. 'And hold a big dance-off for his approval.'

'I'm less worried about the end of the world,' I say, shaking my head, 'and more worried about the end of Quint.'

June leans close. She takes my hand. 'Jack,' she says. 'We're going to get Quint back. We're going to stop Thrull.'

I bang my head against the bars. 'It's been more than an hour. Thrull is probably halfway through his evil ceremony right now. Bet he's all mumbo-jumboing, like –'

'Jack,' June says. 'Stop.'

I sigh. 'What does it matter? I can't be goofy? We're DONE, June.'

'No, Jack. Stop because . . . they're here.'

YOU LOOK LIKE YOU ARE IN NEED OF ASSISTANCE.

chapter
twenty-six

Bardle moves like an old man as he slips down
from Rover and waddles toward us. He looks
the cage up and down, then wraps his hand
around the lock. His eyes close and he focuses.
A moment later, the lock drops. The door swings
open.

'Magic,' Dirk grunts. 'Neat.'

In a flash, I'm out, whipping the Louisville
Slicer over my shoulder. June screams at me to
stop, but I can't. Quint's terrified face flashes
across the inside of my eyelids.

Did you
have anything to
do with this?!

'No,' Bardle says flatly.

I look at him for a long moment. I *have* to believe him – no other choice. I slowly lower the Louisville Slicer. 'Do you know what Thrull is up to? And why he stole my best bud?'

He nods.

'Then why did you deny it?!' I ask. 'We told you about the zombies with their brains sucked out, but you said you knew nothing!'

'Because I had only just begun to suspect that Thrull was a servant of Ṛeżżőch. You must understand – even though we all came here from the same world, we know each other no better than you might know a stranger whom you encounter. I was the first to come to Joe's Pizza after Thrull. I stumbled upon him. He welcomed me. I did not yet realize who he was or what he would do.

'When you mentioned undead humans with their brains removed, my suspicions were raised. I suspected a Tree of Entry. I began to investigate. But I did not know for certain until this very moment.'

I'm steaming.

'Jack, would you like to continue arguing or would you like to save your friend?' Bardle asks. 'And your world?'

'Save his friend and save the world,' June says, jumping in. 'That's his answer: save the friend, save the world. Trust me.'

Dirk is downing a huge bottle of water and the colour is returning to his face. 'So what now?' he asks after he swallows.

'We can get the other monsters from Joe's,' Bardle says. 'They will all take up the fight. Only the insane worship Ŗeżżőcħ.'

I shake my head. There's no time for that. I take quick strides toward Rover.

'Jack, what are you doing?' June asks.

'I'm getting back Quint. I'm stopping Thrull.'

'Well, we're coming!' June exclaims.

'Thrull took Big Mama. We can't all go.'

'Rover can carry the four of us.'

'You cannot stop him alone,' Bardle says.

'Watch me.'

Dirk plants his feet in a wide stance, blocking my way. 'We're coming, bro.'

I tug on Rover's reins and he trots around Dirk and toward the gate. I turn back and give my friends a final look, and then, 'Rover, HEE-YA!'

Rover gallops forward, but suddenly –

The ground trembles. The grass beneath the tree house splits and giant chunks of earth slide and crack. All around the base of the tree, the yard swells and the water in our moat pool splashes.

'What's happening?' Dirk shouts.

Tossed to the ground, I quickly sprint back to my friends, tugging on Rover's collar. We huddle together as the grass explodes –

BURST!

'The Wormungulous! What's he doing here?!'
June asks. She staggers back.

Rover dashes past me and darts over to the
Wormungulous. They sort of wrestle, Rover
hopping all around the other monster. Rover's
neck turns, like he's trying to show the worm
where to go.

Bardle smiles as he sees the creature. 'It is an
Ūň§æṛċœŵ.'

The worm makes a sound like a cow. Like an
underground cow. Remind me – Underground
Cow: great name for a rock band.

The worm dives beneath the surface again.

'Hey, where's he going?' June asks.

'You're messing up my garden, worm!' Dirk
hollers.

The Wormungulous appears again. The tree
tilts to the side and lifts up, out of the ground.
Worm tentacles grab hold of the tree roots like
they're interlocking fingers, connecting with them,
joining, so that soon I can barely see where the
worm ends and the tree begins.

Dirt erupts, filling the air with brown bits that
throw me into a coughing fit. The Wormungulous's
strange worm tentacles now reach and wrap
around the tree's trunk, securing it.

The worm cranes its gigantic head, looking toward us.

I look at this strange new companion in awe. 'Dirk,' I finally say. 'Can you use the pulleys to lift the Weed-B-Gone barrels into the tree house?'

Dirk smirks and flexes. 'What do you think?'

'Good,' I say. 'June, help me load in every monster-fighting weapon we've got. We're going to rescue Quint. We're going to destroy that tree. We're going to stop Thrull. And the Wormungulous is giving us a ride . . .'

chapter twenty-seven

ALL right, team! Let's get these Weed-B-Gone cannons up and running!

The tree house rumbles beneath us as the Wormungulous races across Wakefield.

Dirk – all Captain Masculine – managed to shove every barrel of Weed-B-Gone into our main room and out of sight. His toolbox is open as he works to mount three Super Soakers to the tree house railing. Every minute or so, the worm hits something, the entire tree house jerks, and Dirk bangs his head and shrieks. Finally –

'Super Soakers attached!' Dirk shouts.

'Garden hoses coming!' I call.

June and I rush back and forth, running long coils of garden hose from the barrels to the Super Soakers. As soon as we squeeze those plastic Soaker triggers, oh man – Weed-B-Gone is going to blast out like a jet . . . a jet of tree-obliterating ooze.

But it's all worthless if we don't get there in time to save Quint . . .

Rover leads the way across Wakefield, and the Wormungulous follows, its tail end whipping back and forth, powering us. The Wormungulous's gigantic, thrashing teeth devour anything that threatens to slow us down. It chews through concrete and ploughs through barricades.

We pass known zombie hangouts – zombie hangouts that are now empty. Our middle school, where we found June, months back. The zombies are no more. The grocery store, where we would grab food – not a single zombie.

I soon spot a wall of trees in the distance. The forest looms ahead of us. It seems to be leaking darkness, like the place itself cannot stand light. Evil is in there. Evil, helping *more* evil to enter this world . . .

The Wormungulous weaves around the thickest trees, leaving a trail of splintered wood and ragged earth in its wake. Branches whip against the tree house. Other trees are crushed. Snapped at the base. Ripped from the ground.

In minutes, we travel miles – deep into the heart of the forest. Until far up ahead, I see a glowing light.

The clearing.

The shrieking Tree of Entry.

Bardle grips the railing. 'Slowly, slowly,' he says. 'We do not want to spook Thrull.'

I whistle. Rover slows to a trot, then stops. The worm grinds to a halt.

June hears it first. She looks to me, her face pale with fear. Then Dirk. I hear it, too.

Chanting.

I dash up to the lookout for a better view.
As I peer through the telescope, the thickness
of the tangled forest almost blocks my view.
Almost . . .

Oh no. Quint . . .

chapter twenty-eight

The two longest branches, outlining a giant V against a dark and ferocious sky, are shaking violently. Bright, colourful energy crackles and sparks and rains down on the overgrown grass below.

Beneath the tree, Thrull holds the bestiary high, spewing all sorts of crazy megavillain stuff . . .

With those words, the two huge branches
begin to bend. They lower toward the ground,
then jab into the earth like two blades. I gasp.
The branches are like the door frame, I realize –
and the energy is the door.

The booming voice of Ŗeżžőċħ the Ancient
erupts. High in our tree house, his voice seems
to shake the walls and floors. This voice, its
power – it puts Blarg to shame. Whatever is
beyond that door – it would eat Blarg with a side
of zombie onion rings.

'YESSSS . . . FINISH THE CEREMONY . . . INSERT THE KEY . . . OPEN THE DOOR . . .'

Dirk grips the railing. 'This is messed up.'

'Majorly messed up,' June agrees.

'I'm going down there,' I say.

'And doing what?' June asks.

'I'll get Quint back,' I say. 'I don't know how. But I'll get him back.'

June's eyes light up. 'Good. Go. Distract Thrull. Break the spell or whatever this craziness is,' June says, spinning the Super Soaker. 'And I'll shoot Quint down.'

'No!' Bardle suddenly says. His voice is sharp. 'Let me go. Let me talk to Thrull first.'

I eye Bardle. My understanding of whom to trust and whom not to trust these days has gone way off course. I've learned that I am, apparently, a terrible judge of character in monsters.

I look to June and Dirk. They nod.

'OK, Bardle,' I say. 'We'll go together.'

Bardle scrambles up onto my back. I grip the fire pole. 'Wish us luck.' With that, we slide down to the ground. Bardle scrambles off me and together we dash fifty yards, through the trees, toward the super-scary-death-tree-and-double-megavillains.

The light from the energy door is nearly
blinding. Colours swirl and flow. I'm peering
into a different dimension – and it causes my
stomach to tighten up and fear to flood through
me . . .

As Thrull continues chanting, the bestiary
begins to transform.

'Œþūælő şĕąšmę.'

Thrull's words cause the book to radiate with
an intense, blinding light. It's like I can *sense*
the power of the master inside. The essence of
each monster, charged by Thrull's magic, has
turned the book into a sort of key.

I keep an eye on Quint. He hangs from a Vine-Thingie. He's clearly being saved as an appetizer for Ŗeżżőcħ. Thrull's treating my buddy like he's a jalapeño popper! Nobody treats my buddies like jalapeño poppers!

Bardle bursts into the clearing and shouts, 'Stop this madness!'

Thrull spins around. He smiles at Bardle. A slight grin. 'I'm sorry, but I cannot. I am a servant.'

I watch Quint, dangling like a worm on a hook. He lifts his head, looking out at Bardle. I stay hidden behind the tree, just barely peeking out.

'Do not be a fool!' Bardle barks. His ancient voice cracks. 'Why destroy this place? It is our new home!'

'I care nothing for the pitiful home of humans! I will sit beside Ŗeżżőcħ on a throne! Together, we will rule all! Devour all! Now, no more talk,' Thrull says. 'I must finish.'

Thrull lifts the hockey stick up, cracks a broken grin, and *slams* it into the ground. It erupts.

A circular wave of earth rolls outward. Bardle is lifted off his feet and knocked into the air.

I jump, leaping over the rolling earth. I land on solid ground, draw my blade, and stomp forward.

Thrull has returned to his incantations. 'Ćðñó bėŝðmĕ mūćħő.'

OK.

Now it's my turn.

This Thrull character might be just fine at giving the business to his fellow monsters. But he's never tangled with Jack Sullivan, seventh-grade Post-Apocalyptic Action Hero and cool guy extraordinaire.

Thrull ignores me. He continues chanting furious incantations.

'THRULL!' I bark. 'I SAID STOP THE MUMBO-JUMBOING AND DROP THE KEY!'

Bardle appears beside me. He's dazed. He places a hand on my shoulder and eyes the surging, swirling energy. 'I'm afraid the ceremony is nearly complete . . .'

We need to distract Thrull from completing the ceremony! But my cracking, high-pitched voice ain't cutting it . . .

Then suddenly, from above . . .

Music erupts from our new tree house
speakers. Booming, bass-heavy June tunes.
The music is cranked up so loud the speakers
are practically jumping. The pop songs fill the
forest. Beyoncé might just save planet Earth!

I see Thrull's shoulder twist. His head jerks.
He's struggling to finish the ceremony. He trips
over his words and the portal cries and screams.
And at last –

'NOW, JUNE!' I shout. 'NOW! NOW! NOW!'

I hear a *WHOOSH* sound and a blast of Weed-B-Gone arcs over my head. Thrull spins and watches as the weed killer blasts the Vine-Thingies, freeing Quint!

In a flash, Quint's up, running toward me. I hear trees cracking and breaking and I feel the ground tremble as the Wormungulous snakes its way closer and the tree house looms above us.

Ŗeżżőcħ's voice calls from the beyond.

'FINISHHHH . . . THEEEE . . . CEREMONyyyyy . . .!'

Thrull's eyes are wide as he sees the tree house entering the clearing and the Wormungulous beneath it.

This is working! We've stopped the ceremony! And Quint's escaping! Thanks, Beyoncé!

But then Quint slows down. His lab coat whips about him and his feet begin to drag. 'Quint, what are you doing?!' I shout.

I don't understand – is he, like, possessed? Thrull storms toward him, grabs Quint with one massive paw, and lifts him up into the air. 'YOU AND YOUR FRIENDS WILL PAY!'

The bestiary key glows in Thrull's hand. The portal burns brighter and brighter. Thrull bellows out the incantations. A crescendo is building. The energy inside the door swirls. An image appears. A figure. Its shape is shifting, altering. One instant, I see wings. The next, furious spikes. A moment later, I glimpse what appears to be a bony tail.

Its form is indefinable.

This is it.

Ŗeżżőch the Ancient.

The Destructor of Worlds.

His voice booms: *'INSERT THE KEY . . . OPEN THE DOOR . . . THIS WORLD WILL BE MINE . . .'*

No, no, no, no. He can't have this world! I'm not signing off on that!

And then, at the last possible moment –

Quint looks to me. He grins. *Hey, it's another devious Quint grin!* Quint's hands dart into his lab coat, he yanks something from his waist, and –

chapter
twenty-nine

BOOMERANG BURST!

I reel back, throwing my arm over my eyes. Another of Quint's patented BOOMerangs – the weapon that goes BOOM!

The bright light fades and I see everything unfold as if in slow motion. Quint is dashing toward me. Thrull is behind him, knees in the mud, holding his eyes. He jerks from side to side.

And in Quint's arms: the bestiary! He stole it back from Thrull!

Quint shoves the book under his arm like he's a star football player (first and last time you'll ever hear someone describe Quint that way).

The door begins to dim. Ŗeżżõċh lets out a long, bloodcurdling shriek. The tree shakes and the branches lash out.

The door is closing. The energy fading. The light dissipating.

Quint slides to a stop as he nears the tree house.

Quint noodles that for about 0.7 seconds, then proclaims it 'Fantastic news!'

A crackling, hissing sound fills the air and a final piercing cry erupts from the portal. And then, with a sizzling *SNAP*, the portal closes.

I breathe a titanic-sized sigh of relief. This world-devouring dude's entry has been halted. A smell hangs in the air – that flowery, earthy smell you get after a summer rain shower.

'We did it!' Quint says. 'The portal's closed! And we have the bestiary!'

'So what do we do with him?' I say, watching Thrull continue to stumble around, covering his eyes.

Bardle shakes his head. 'I do not believe it is entirely over.'

Quint eyes Bardle. 'Jack, *he's* on our side now?'

'Yes, Quint. Catch up. You miss a lot in two hours when those two hours are the climax of a battle for the future of the world.'

'Look,' Bardle says.

We all turn to the tree. There's a soft crackling and a few small bursts of light. The door appears again – just for one quick instant – and the fading, crying voice of Ṛeżżóċh delivers one final order.

'THRULLLLL . . . FINISH THEMMMMM . . .
AND RETRIEVE THE KEYYYY . . .'

And with that, the door blinks away.

Thrull no longer looks defeated – no, he looks like he's on his last legs, forced to demonic desperation. He begins laughing. Softly, at first, and then louder. Louder and louder until a cackling, high-pitched, hideous howl fills the forest.

He stares at us.

No.

Not us.

Me.

Directly at me.

'You have not won, Jack Sullivan,' he growls. 'You have only delayed the coming of Ŗeżżóčħ.'

Thrull's eyes snap shut. His head raises to the sky. A quick flow of strange, foreign enchantments tumble from his mouth.

'ßëńşő čhę un sőǧnő cosi ńœ rïtornì mài þį̊ů.'

His voice grows louder and louder.

'Oh no,' Bardle says. His voice is barely a whisper.

'What *oh no*?' I ask.

'It is a unification spell. It binds two beings together.'

'Well, let's stop him!' I spin around, calling to June. 'June, more tunes! Something *real* annoying!'

'It is too late,' Bardle says. 'It is done.'

It is **never** too late! Haven't you ever seen an action movie? *Indiana Jones? Ghostbusters?* Anything? There's always one last thing to be done!

Jack, what are you talking about?

I dunno. I may have lost my mind a bit.

Thrull's insane incantations finish with a few final words in English. A few final *terrifying* words: 'I, servant of Ṛeżżőcħ, wish to join you. TOGETHER, WE WILL RETRIEVE THE KEY AND BRING Ṛeżżőcħ INTO THIS WORLD!'

And then, the most horrific thing, well, ever

happens. Thrull raises his arms. He cackles like a mad, giggling demon and gives me a final look before his eyes shut and he roars, *'TAKE ME!'*

The Vine-Thingies, thousands of them, begin to swirl and spin, forming a terrible tornado, twisting and braiding and intertwining themselves together until they've formed one gigantic mouth. The mouth opens wide and –

SWALLOW!

'It swallowed him whole!' Quint gasps.

And for the second time in about two minutes and nineteen seconds, the tree changes. It morphs and it grows and it becomes more alive than any tree should ever be. The roots rip from the ground. Branches turn to hands, pressing against the earth, forcing the tree free.

The branches reach up and tear a mouth in the trunk of the tree. The horrific wooden mouth bellows out 'SO I CAN SEE' as the hands rip eyeholes in the bark.

'THAT'S BETTER!' the voice roars – and the voice is muddy and earthy and wet but it is unmistakably the voice of Thrull.

The tree continues pulling itself from the soil. The earth quakes, and dirt and soil fill the air. When it clears, we're staring at . . .

Thrull the Tree Beast!

chapter thirty

Jack! Get up here!

Quint scales the ladder. Bardle hops on my back like an oversized Yoda, and we follow. June and Dirk greet us at the top.

'We need to get the bestiary far away from Thrull!' June exclaims. 'If he gets it back, he can do the key thing again!'

Bardle steps forward. 'He will come after us. He is too powerful. We must make a stand.'

'How?' Quint asks.

LEAD THE FIEND BACK TO JOE'S. THE MANY MONSTERS THERE WILL TAKE UP THE FIGHT. TOGETHER, YOUR KIND AND MY KIND, FIGHTING AS ONE – THAT IS OUR BEST CHANCE OF DEFEATING HIM.

'And we've got the Weed-B-Gone Super Soakers!' I exclaim. 'Combine all that – maybe we can cut this tree down to size.'

'You sure your monster buddies aren't loyal to Ŗeżżőcħ?' June asks Bardle. 'Or Thrull?'

'I am certain,' Bardle says. 'Thrull cloaked his evil stench. I was a fool for not noticing. But no one else there emits the scent – I'm sure of it.'

Behind us, the earth quakes. Thrull is continuing to rip himself from the earth. He'll be upon us soon.

I reach for the bestiary. 'OK. I'll take it. I'll ride Rover to Joe's and tell the monsters to prepare for battle.'

Quint grips it tight. 'No. I'll go.'

Behind us, Thrull continues to pull himself loose. The earth rolls and quakes.

'Quint, there's no time!' I say. 'It's too dangerous. You guys stay in the tree house; it's safer. I'll take it.'

'Jack, let me do this!' Quint barks. 'You can't do everything!'

'Yes, I can!'

I eye my friends. Am I being scolded? Like a little kid! And scolded for trying to save them?

No.

No, I'm being scolded for not trusting them. For not placing my faith in them, the way they've placed their faith in me.

I know it.

I can't do it all.

Friends are important. Family is important. Maybe the most important thing. But even a Post-Apocalyptic Action Hero can't keep them safe all the time.

Looking into Quint's eyes, I realize that I *have* to let him do this. He must carry the bestiary alone.

I feel a nudge at my side. I see Rover, eyes wide, eager to help. 'Rover,' I say. 'Take Quint to Joe's, OK? And Bardle.'

Quint scrambles up on Rover's back. I lift Bardle and he wraps his long, strange fingers around Quint's shoulders.

'Jack, slow Thrull down,' Bardle says. 'Give us time to get to Joe's and prepare my friends.'

'On it. No problem,' I say. 'And Quint?'

'Yes?'

I grab his hand. We shake once, hard. 'You got this, buddy.'

Quint grins, and then Rover leaps. They hit the ground and my monster dog takes off into the woods. An instant later there's a tremendous *KRASH* as Thrull the Tree Beast stands opposite us.

Monstrous feet of trunk and root take tremendous, earth-shattering steps as Thrull storms past us. He's focused on Rover, Quint, and Bardle – and the bestiary.

'Wormungulous, go, go, go!' I shout. 'Follow that big ol' tree monster!'

Thrull's Vine-Thingies dart at us, swinging and slashing through the air.

'LAY ON THE SOAKERS!' Dirk shouts,
squeezing the flimsy plastic trigger. Neon-green
Weed-B-Gone erupts from the nozzles and the
Vine-Thingies snap back. Steam pours off them.

Thrull the Tree Beast raises a heavy fist of
vine and wood.

'Duck!' I shriek, and the fist swings through
the air, tremendously powerful, but slow – like
a wrecking ball. The Wormungulous DIVES into
the ground, and Thrull's massive punch just
barely connects –

KRASH!

DE-ROOFED!

Splinters of wood rain down. One jagged piece lands, dead centre, in my PlayStation.

'HE BROKE THE PLAYSTATION!' I roar. 'I'VE HAD ENOUGH OF THIS! HOSES!'

Dashing back out onto the deck, we man the cannons. The tree house bobs and shifts and jumps as we race across town.

Vine-Thingies lash out as the Wormungulous keeps pace with Thrull the Tree Beast. We're battling side to side, like in an olden-days pirate fight.

I grab the walkie and bark, 'Quint, we're coming toward Joe's – hard and fast!'

A second later, Quint comes over the walkie: 'We're still riding Rover! We need more time! Slow him down!'

HOW? He doesn't need to follow roads! He just STOMPS. STOMPS WITH TREE LEGS!

'THE FEET!' June calls out. 'SOAK THE FEET!'

We tilt the Soakers down, showering his tremendous trunk legs with Weed-B-Gone. His feet, all root and bark, seem to burn. He slows. The Wormungulous races ahead and we burst out of the woods.

We're back on the streets of Wakefield, charging down long, wide avenues, the Wormungulous knocking cars aside and blasting through houses.

Thrull ploughs through Comically Speaking, the local comic book joint. Pages flutter in the air. Vintage action figures – smashed! I nearly faint from the horror! A cardboard cutout of Wolverine is crushed beneath Thrull's muddy feet. Not cool, Thrull . . .

We grab every single weapon we have. Every one of Quint's crazy creations that we used to

capture the essence of the monsters now filling
the bestiary. And we unload . . .

But it's not enough.

We're turning onto Main Street.

I see it directly ahead of us, the scene of our
final showdown: Joe's Pizza.

chapter thirty-one

Joe's Pizza sits below us. I see no sign of Quint. No sign of Rover or Bardle. I buzz into the walkie and say, 'Quint, I'm sorry, but we're here.'

Silence.

Then, a moment later, the front door to Joe's Pizza flies open and –

Whoa, OK. Quint's like a general in a monster army now. Right on.

Bardle steps out last, gasping. He catches my eye and nods. I return the gesture.

A deafening collective monster roar fills the air – and then they're suddenly scaling Thrull the Tree Beast!

'Time to rumble!' Dirk says. He leaps from the tree house, hits the ground, and rolls. He's instantly up, throwing tremendous punches. Tentacle branches come for him, but Dirk grabs the monstrous wood arms, twisting them, punching them and breaking them.

'GET! BENT!' Dirk yells as he grabs one branch and snaps it against his knee. It shatters with a violent, splintering crack.

June and I lay on the Super Soakers. The sharp scent of the Weed-B-Gone fills the air. The fumes are blinding but we continue blasting.

Thrull the Tree Beast unleashes a deafening roar, then shakes his wooden limbs, sending monsters spiralling through the air.

Thrull stomps toward June and me. The Wormungulous slithers backward.

'YOU. WILL. PAY,' Thrull roars.

'Jack, down!' June says as she slams into me, tackling me to the floor in the nick of time. Thrull's hand grabs hold of the Soakers. His wooden fingers tighten and –

HOSE RIP!

My stomach sinks. The Soakers are gone. I had
hoped if the monsters could keep Thrull busy, we
could do him in with the Weed-B-Gone. But that
plan is out the window. And worse than that –

The bestiary!

I spot Quint gripping the book, darting around
like he's trying to avoid a swarm of bees, but a

horde of Vine-Thingies quickly hunt him down.
They grab hold, yanking him into the air.

'YES! THE BESTIARY KEY!' Thrull roars.

As Quint is lifted, he flings the book. It lands
in the hands of a thin, many-armed monster.
The monster swings from a tree branch. Thrull
swipes at it, but the many-armed monster tosses
the bestiary to the next friendly beast.

It's a game of hot potato.

But it's a game we can't win. It won't last.
Thrull is too strong.

'I'm going to help!' June says, leaping over the
side. She lands, shouts, 'TO ME!' and the book
drops into her arms. June – quick, athletic,
wielding her half-busted spear – slices up Vine-
Thingies as she darts around with the book.

'Dirk!' I shout. 'Get up here!'

In moments, he's coming over the side. 'How
much of that Weed-B-Gone do we have left?' I
quickly ask.

Dirk grabs hold of a Vine-Thingie. 'Five
barrels,' he says as he casually rips the vine in
half. 'But without the Soakers, what can we do?
We can't carry it. And it's too heavy to launch
with the catapult.'

There's a *KRAK* outside. The Wormungulous

bellows and we're suddenly sent stumbling through the door and into the tree house. I plough into the poker table. A second later, there's a tremendous bang as something *very heavy* lands on me. I sit up, rubbing my head.

It's my space marine armour suit. An idea begins to form . . .

'Dirk,' I say. 'Help me suit up!'

Dirk looks at me like I'm nuts. Fair enough. I probably am.

chapter thirty-two

'June, up here!' Dirk shouts. 'Throw me the bestiary!'

I watch as June attempts to keep the book away from Thrull. A Vine-Thingie quickly snaps out and snatches her into the air.

As she's spun around, she manages to hurl the book to another monster: a short, six-legged thing. And at last, the book is heaved up to Dirk. He hands it to me. 'You sure about this, bro?'

'I'm sure. Just get me chained to those Weed-B-Gone barrels, or else – well, or else it's been nice knowing you . . .'

HERE IT IS, THRULL! HERE'S YOUR BESTIARY! YOUR KEY! COME AND GET IT!

The giant tree monster stares down at me. Wood splinters as his eyes narrow.

Dirk hurriedly uses Rover's chain and a bunch of old bike locks to loop the barrels together and hook them to my suit. I check the plastic pockets: yep, I've got everything I need.

Thrull's immense hand opens.

'Are the barrels hooked on?' I shout.

'Almost!' Dirk says.

I hear the bike locks banging and clanging.

My knees are practically knocking together as Thrull's hand lowers.

'Hurry, Dirk! He's almost got me!'

'Hurrying, bro!'

I gulp.

And then, an instant before the massive wooden hand seizes me, I hear a *CLICK* and Dirk slaps the suit and says, 'GOOD TO GO!'

I want to shut my eyes.

But I don't.

I stare down Thrull as his monstrous hand scoops me up . . .

The giant barrels of weed killer dangle from my space marine suit, swinging and clanging in the air. Thrull's body bends backward and the tree cracks. The mouth opens wide.

REŻŻÓCH THE ANCIENT, THIS WORLD WILL SOON BE YOURS!

As Thrull places me into his mouth, I manage to fling the book backward, away from him. Thrull's wooden eyes go wide, but it's too late.

I tumble into the monster's mouth. His giant wooden teeth slam into the barrels. Crushing them. Weed killer bursts from the busted metal.

I'm falling.

I see nothing but darkness as I tumble through the inside of this strange, hollow tree. The metal barrels knock against me. I hear weed killer sloshing out, splashing everywhere.

Reaching into the suit, I manage to pull a single TNT-brand-triple-explosive bottle rocket from my pocket. As I plummet, I scrape the wick against the barrel. It sparks and the bottle rocket lights up the inner darkness of the hollow, monstrous tree.

With one powerful swing, I jab the bottle rocket into the side of one barrel. And I brace myself . . .

I finally hit the ground inside of the tree. My knees slam into my chest, and it takes a second to catch my breath before I can stand. The barrels crash into the ground all around me and the weed killer continues to rush out.

Thrull the Tree Beast shrieks! Wood snaps and cracks around me. At my feet, jutting out of the barrel, the bottle rocket burns.

Weed killer pools around my feet. Looking up, I see it pouring down the inside of the tree.

Sorry, Thrull, but in this dimension, we've got something called 'fireworks'. And they're a blast.

The bottle rocket wick is down to nothing. Smoke clouds my vision. I look away, shut my eyes tight, and . . .

The bottle rocket EXPLODES, setting off a chain reaction. Every barrel blows with it. I hope that this suit is strong enough to save me . . .

The trunk of the tree shatters completely. The monsters leap off, running and diving for safety.

My body is *rocked* – a tidal wave of explosive energy rips through me, hurling me from the inside of the tree. Only the space marine suit keeps me from being blown to bits.

Thrull howls. His voice, twisted and pained, echoes as the tree melts away to nothing. Soon, it is completely gone – disintegrated.

In the end, only Thrull remains.

chapter thirty-three

I now have a general understanding of what it might feel like to be inside an exploding dishwasher: wet, messy, a tiny bit fun, but a great relief when it's over.

Dirk and June help me out of the armour. I'm soaking wet, dripping with maybe-probably-toxic weed killer.

'Hope you don't turn into some sort of Swamp Thing monster,' June says.

'Would you still be my friend?'

'Your Swamp Thing friend? Ehh, probably not.'

'That's messed up!' I say with a laugh.

And then I realize – I can't be saying things with a laugh! Not yet.

We need to deal with Thrull.

'He's gone!' Quint exclaims.

Where Thrull was lying a moment earlier, I now see only wet leaves and cracked cement.

And the bestiary. The bestiary lies alone.

Bardle hobbles toward us, the other monsters close behind. Some have been hurt by the now-dead tree's monstrous limbs. But many have smiles on their faces.

'So . . . where did Thrull go?' June asks. 'He just, like, magic-trick vanished.'

'The beasts that serve Ṛeżżȯcḣ are not defeated easily,' Bardle says.

I grit my teeth. 'So he got away . . .'

Bardle nods. 'For now. But he will never return to our pizza parlour. I promise you that. And it would take him a very long time to plant and feed another tree portal. I suspect you will never hear The Shrieking again.'

Very slowly, Quint bends down and picks up the book. I half expect a bolt of lightning to strike him down. But nothing crazy happens – he just holds it gently in his hands, then taps on the cover.

'Bardle,' Quint says. 'Please, tell us every-thing you know about Ṛeżżȯcḣ the Ancient. About his servants.'

Dirk suddenly comes sliding down the pole. ''Cause we need to stop that Ŗeżżóċħ for good.'

Bardle shakes his head. 'I will tell you all that I know. But stopping Ŗeżżóċħ forever? He will be a threat to this world always. His servants are relentless.'

'We are, too,' I say. 'At night I can never –'

'Relentless, Jack,' Quint says. 'Not *restless*.'

Before I can think of a quippy comeback, the ground at our feet begins to tremble. The Wormungulous bellows, then dives beneath the surface of Joe's parking lot, plunging the tree's roots into the ground. The earth splits and the Wormungulous disappears entirely.

Um . . .

Dude? Wormungulous? We sorta still need you . . .

To get our home back, like, **home**.

'So . . . he's gone,' June says, shooting me a look. 'Just like that. And now our tree house is stuck next to the pizza place?'

'Are you glaring at me?' I ask.

'Yes, I'm glaring,' June says.

'Why are you glaring?'

'Because it's kinda *all your fault!* You're the hero, Jack! And when things go wrong, the hero's the one responsible.'

'Correction,' I say, holding up a finger. 'We're *all* the heroes, June. Quint led an army of monsters, you swung from vines like Tarzan, and Dirk hulked out. All I had to do was fall through a tree. Any dumb idiot could do that.'

Quint is practically shaking with happiness. 'Friends, that means we can hook up a zip line right into the restaurant!'

'Yes!' I say. 'The zip line can run over a big pile of dough balls so we just – *poof* – drop and land, like a ball pit. We will be . . . ULTIMATE REGULARS!'

I grin at that thought. My friends rush inside to celebrate. I hang back for a moment, just standing. Thinking.

Happy to have saved everyone.

Even more happy that we did it as a team.

I hear a long moaning sound. Zombies. They seem to be watching from the end of the street. I see Alfred. He's 'alive' and safe forever from the zombie-eating tree. He'll be all right on his own now. So long, butler.

Just before I enter, I spot something on the ground. My zombie-noggin-conking hockey stick. Thrull's crutch. 'I'll be taking that back, Thrull,' I say.

Two hours later, we're still celebrating. Quint's on his eleventh free soda. 'Regulars get free soda,' he declares. Quint's so happy to be a regular that he's just making up new regular rules as he goes.

It's good.

We have friends.

More friends.

Monster friends.

'Jack,' Bardle says. 'This is our world now, too – and we must share it. Repair it. To do that, we must find more humans, and more monsters.'

I grin. Y'know what . . .

Pages from the Bestiary

Iris opens to allow monster verbal communication (roars, shrieks, howls).

One single, massive eyeball.

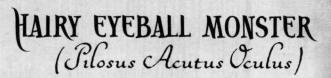

HAIRY EYEBALL MONSTER
(Pilosus Acutus Oculus)

DATA (Quint's best approximations):
Length: 90 feet long
Weight: 1.3 tons
Speed: 45 mph on open ground

When angered, hair stands on end, forming razor-sharp quills.

QUINT NOTES: The Hairy Eyeball Monster has the ability to fire its quills at an enemy with tremendous force. Maximum quill launch distance unknown.
LOCATION: Old South Graveyard
PRINCIPAL ATTACK: Needle onslaught
STRENGTHS: Rolling ability makes for easy, unobstructed travel and pursuit
TEMPERAMENT: Grave

289

PUKE BUG KING
(Rex Putidus Insectus)

DATA (Quint's best approximations):
Length: Adjustable
Weight: 749 pounds
Speed: No clue. Hopefully slow. Because
if not, that's doubly scary...

Body formed
from hundreds
of thousands of
monster insects
joining together.

Emits a deafening series
of clicking, clacking,
and hissing noises – the
result of thousands upon
thousands of monster insects
communicating at once.

Releases a sweet, overpowering stench.

Facial features evident.

QUINT NOTES: Combination of many different insects, formed together to create a 'King Bug'. This monster's full abilities, powers, composition, and anatomy are almost a complete mystery.

KNOWN HABITATS: June's neighbours' house (the Gradwohls)

PRINCIPAL ATTACK: Being totally revolting, insanely horrifying, and generally nightmarish

STRENGTHS: Can paralyse others with fear

WEAKNESSES: Best guess? Citronella-and-bug-spray-flamethrower

TEMPERAMENT: Not pleasant

Acknowledgments

Ahh, the acknowledgments.

This is always the hard part! For a big illustrated book like this to work, it requires so many people working so hard and doing their jobs so well. First, Douglas Holgate, for illustrating the crud out of this book – and for going above and beyond over and over again. My wonderful editor, Leila Sales, who is smarter than smart and more patient than any person should be. If I were half the writer she is, I'd have better adjectives than 'smart' and 'patient' at my fingertips, but alas . . . Jim Hoover, for taking a weird manuscript and instinctively knowing how to make it an actual book. And of course, Ken Wright – thank you for everything. Bridget Hartzler and everyone else in Viking's wonderful publicity and marketing department – thank you for working hard and having fun with this!

Dan Lazar, my agent, for every single last thing. Torie Doherty-Munro, for putting up with my silly questions and inane requests. Kassie Evashevski at UTA for trying so hard to make this more than just a book.

My good friends, whom I always turn to when I'm stuck; the friends that provide me with hugely long group texts full of ideas: Chris Amaru, Geoff Baker, Mando Calrissian, Matt McArdle, Chewy Ryan, Marty Strandberg, Ben Murphy.

And more than anyone – thank you to my wonderful, delightful, darling wife Alyse. Thanks for understanding why I drink nine cups of coffee a day. Thanks for understanding that I just *need* to go for walks at 3 a.m. because some plot hang-up has me mystified. Thanks for letting me sleep in when I'm just fried from deadlines. Thanks for being the best. Thanks for letting me love you.

Are you still reading this?

Get outta here!

Go slay a monster.

MAX BRALLIER!

(maxbrallier.com) is the author of more than thirty book and games. He writes both children's books and adult books, including the Galactic Hot Dogs series and the pick-your-own-path adventure *Can YOU Survive the Zombie Apocalypse?* He has written books for licensed properties including *Adventure Time, Regular Show, Steven Universe, Uncle Grandpa,* and *Poptropica.*

Under the pen name Jack Chabert, he is the creator and author of the Eerie Elementary series for Scholastic Books as well as the author of the *New York Times* bestselling graphic novel *Poptropica: Book 1: Mystery of the Map.* In the olden days, he worked in the marketing department at St. Martin's Press. Max lives in New York City with his wife, Alyse, who is way too good for him.

Follow Max on Twitter @MaxBrallier.

The author building his own tree house as a kiddo. This puppy was NOT seriously armed to the teeth.

DOUGLAS HOLGATE!

(skullduggery.com.au) has been a freelance
comic book artist and illustrator based in Melbourne,
Australia, for more than ten years. He's illustrated
books for publishers such as HarperCollins, Penguin
Random House, Hachette, and Simon & Schuster,
including the Planet Tad series, *Cheesie Mack*, *Case
File 13*, and *Zoo Sleepover*.

Douglas has illustrated comics for Image,
Dynamite, Abrams, and Penguin Random House.
He's currently working on the self-published series
Maralinga, which received grant funding from the
Australian Society of Authors and the Victorian
Council for the Arts, as well as the all-ages graphic
novel *Clem Hetherington and the Ironwood Race*,
published by Scholastic Graphix, both cocreated
with writer Jen Breach.

Follow Douglas on Twitter @douglasbot.

Jack Sullivan, June Del Toro, Quint Baker,
Dirk Savage, Rover – and a whole bunch
of monsters – will return!

Find out how it all began
in Jack's first adventure.

It's TOTAL MONSTER ZOMBIE CHAOS
and Jack and his friends are . . .